To:
Chl...

Happy Reading

A. Bate

I was a Primary School teacher for thirty-nine years, the last fifteen of these as Head Teacher.

Throughout my career I have taught Creative Writing to older Primary School children. Reading and writing have always been my pastimes.

Now retired, I live in St. Helens, Merseyside. I am married with two sons and five grandchildren. In retirement I like playing with my grandchildren, walking, golf, travel, amateur dramatics and I'm a National Trust member.

The Scaretaker

For my wife, Ann. Also Steven, Stuart, Natascha, Anne-Marie
and the grandchildren.

Allan Bate

The Scaretaker

Nightingale Books

NIGHTINGALE PAPERBACK

A CIP catalogue record for this title is available from the British Library.

ISBN 978 1 907552 19 9

Nightingale Books is an imprint of Pegasus Elliot Mackenzie Publishers Ltd.

www.pegasuspublishers.com

First Published in 2011

Nightingale Books
Sheraton House Castle Park
Cambridge England

Printed & Bound in Great Britain

Disclaimer

All the characters in this book are fictitious, and any resemblance to actual persons living or dead, is purely coincidental.

One

I was never one to be told what to do. Nobody bothered me much at school because I just didn't care about their silly school rules. Nobody could make me do something if I didn't want to. Teachers knew that. They knew I didn't care. They knew I wouldn't do much work because I didn't like being there, doing all that writing and reading and answering questions and all that stuff. I'd sooner play on my *Sony PlayStation* at home, but my mum wouldn't let me. She said I had to go to school and "get from under her feet". She said she had to put up with my messing at home for the rest of the day, so why should she have to see me all day long.

Summer term had just started. I'd been excluded from school. I had to stay at home. My mum had been angry. She said I had to stay in for the rest of the day and occupy myself. She said she didn't see why she should see to me when I couldn't behave in school. She threatened to take my *Sony PlayStation* off me and ground me for a week. But I knew she wouldn't do that because then she'd have to find things for me to do. I knew she couldn't be bothered with that. It would cause her too much trouble. I started scattering all my models and throwing my football cards across the room. I kept shouting, 'I want to go out! I want to go out!' over and over. In the end she'd given in and said, 'Go on! Get out of my sight! But don't go anywhere near that bloomin' school!' She'd been in the front room with her friend drinking cans of beer.

I didn't care. Nothing fussed me. But that afternoon in the derelict Oxford Gospel Hall, I got the shock of my life. There was a man, an old man, sitting on an upside down milk crate in the middle of the empty room. He was reading a newspaper.

I was by myself. Not even Chelsea was with me. She was in school like everyone else.

He was just sitting there in the gloom reading his paper. A shaft of sunlight suddenly shone through the tall, end window, making specks of dust dance in the air and lighting him up like a spotlight does to pop stars. Like all of the other windows, the small glass panels had been broken. Scattered all across the floor were mortar, broken glass, stones, bricks.

He was a well built man. His skin was yellowy and saggy. There was a smell of tobacco smoke but it wasn't like the thick, choking smell of cigarettes in our house. It was more like when someone smokes a pipe.

I was just standing there. Very still. I thought he hadn't noticed me. I turned to go and a small piece of glass crunched under my shoe. The man looked up. He smiled at me. Looking down again, he carried on reading his newspaper. It made me angry to see him sitting there in my secret place. I picked up a stone and threw it across the room at him. It bounced on the floorboards and flew past him into a dark corner. Pigeons rose and flapped in the gloom above. The man lowered his paper and looked hard at me, but he didn't move.

I shouted, 'Get out of here, you bloody old tramp! This is our place. Get out! Get out!'

I ran back across to the boarded window, pushed back one of the planks and clambered out, back into the grounds which were overgrown with weeds.

I thought he was an old tramp squatting in our secret den. But this couldn't be further from the truth, as I was soon to find out. In time I'd soon see his effect on me.

The old Oxford Gospel Hall had always been our secret den and favourite place to play. When I say 'Our', I mean mainly Chelsea and me. I'd been there with Tom and Joe and Adrian, but mostly I went with Chelsea. Chelsea never argued with me. She just said what we shouldn't do, if she thought it was wrong. My mum said, 'She puts up with you, you little sod.' The others, very often fell out with me and sometimes wouldn't let me join in their games. They said, 'You always spoil it! You always end up fighting!' But they still sometimes have to let me play because they're frightened of me, because I can scrap any of them. So, I mostly went to the Hall with Chelsea. But nobody at school says Chelsea is my girlfriend, because she isn't. Since Jacob Jackson said it and I had a fight with him and made his nose and lip bleed, nobody else has ever said it. Not to the Mighty Craig!

My mum said that the Gospel Hall was very old, that it had been built in the last century. The stone date tablet above the big, oak doors at the front says 1908. She said it was derelict and dangerous and was falling down. She said she remembered it when it was a carpet warehouse five years ago.

'Don't you ever go near the place,' she said. 'One day the roof will collapse and kill some poor, little beggar. Perhaps then they'll knock it down! I'm surprised it hasn't been demolished and made into another car park!'

But I liked going to the Gospel Hall because it was dangerous and like an *Indiana Jones* adventure where the great explorer, Craig, could find things and escape from falling boulders and snakes and spiders and things. It was quiet and secret and had lots of things you could climb on and lots of things you could break or wreck with nobody to tell you off. It had a pointed roof with slates missing and tall windows with small panes. Along one side the windows were arched and pointed like a proper church. Chelsea told me they were called lances or lancets or something. She knows lots of things and works on the computer to find all kinds of things. She's a brainy head and helps me with my work in class, sometimes.

Miss Denton sometimes says, 'Chelsea, will you give Craig a hand with some words?' But sometimes I get annoyed because I don't know what to do and nobody will explain properly so I rip up the paper or screw it up and throw it across the room at Jacob Jackson because he gets on my nerves and is always winding me up. So when I get him back he always tells the teacher. And I get done! Every time! Even when I've only got my own back when that Jacob's been calling me names. Miss Denton says I don't know what to do in the work because I don't listen. But listening is boring!

Anyway, I always listen to Chelsea when we're out playing together because she listens to me and nobody else around our street will play with me.

There is a low wall all round the Gospel Hall with tall, spiky railings. They're very sharp and pointed at the top. They've been painted green but are rusty in lots of places. David Jennings told us that a boy had slipped once trying to climb over and the pointed railing went straight through his stomach and out through his back. It makes me think of *Indiana Jones* in that dark cave before the big boulder rolls at him and he sees the skeletons with spikes straight through them.

But we know where there are railings missing near the back and we can slip through easily into the grounds. The grounds around the Hall are great. The grass is long and there are nettles and clumps of tall plants with purple heads and long leaves. They're great because you can make dens in them. If you snap them off and strip their leaves and purple heads, they make great spears to throw at people.

I didn't like the strange man being in there. So I ran fast, the long grass slapping my shins and ankles. Stopping suddenly on a small pile of bricks, I picked one up. Looking all around, I pulled up the hood on my *Nike* sweat top. I turned and threw at the nearest window. I was angry that someone was sitting in our private place. The brick smashed through a small pane of glass. Laughing out loud, I punched the air with my fist, jumped and kicked my way through a bed of nettles and slipped out through the gap in the railings.

Two

I'd been to the Gospel Hall with Chelsea on Saturday afternoon. Picking up stones I'd been about to smash a few windows, then…

'Don't do that, Craig!' she said, 'you'll have people reporting us. Then they might stop us going in. Besides, this is our secret place, so why wreck it? Let's go in and see if that man's there...'

If anyone else had said 'Don't', Adrian or my mum or my teacher, I'd have probably thrown the stone all the more. But Chelsea was my best friend, my only real friend, and I usually listened to her. I don't know why, except that she seemed to have some hold over me. Might be because I didn't want to lose her as a friend. She was like something that whispered in my head. Sometimes when I hear whispers in my head they tell me to do bad things. But Chelsea was like something in my head telling me not to do bad things, and to do good things.

Keeping my hood up, I ran across to the secret entrance. Sliding back the plank, I held it and let Chelsea clamber inside. Then, easily, I slipped through the gap and pushed back the plank.

At first it was very black and I couldn't see a thing. It was like the time we went on a school trip to *White Scar Caves*. Our whole group had walked down long, low tunnels hunched and bent like the Orcs and Goblins in *Lord of The Rings*. We followed the underground stream. Going into a huge cavern we saw pointed rocks hanging down from the roof. I can't remember what they were called. Then the man told us all to stand still and not move a muscle because he was going to turn out all the electric lights. He threw the switch. All the girls screamed. Adrian made whooping ghost noises, but I started making them first. Anyway, I tried looking at my hand and held it in front of my face. It was so dark, I couldn't see anything. For a few seconds inside the Hall, it was just like that. Then the light from the high end window got into our eyes and we began to see shapes and objects.

Standing in the middle on a wooden bench, Chelsea was scanning the room,

'Well, I can't see anybody. No old man in here.' Her voice went round and round and up to the ceiling, echoing from the timber beams which looked like the skeleton bones of a fish.

'He was just there sitting on that crate,' I said, jumping over a pile of rubble.

'He must have moved on. Found a better place to go,' said Chelsea, examining a roll of dusty cloth. Unrolling it on the wooden floorboards, a little cloud of dust made her cough. Then we could see it was a banner of some sort.

'It's hessian and it's got writing stitched into it.'

'What's flippin' hessian?'

'It's a cloth. Like sack material.'

Opening it out fully, we could make out the faded blue letters. It said *"Oxford Gospel Hall 1952"*. There was a picture of Jesus with arms stretched out, a ring at the top of his head and a lamp in his left hand. Chelsea read the words under it, *"I am The Light Of The World"*. It was all stitched neatly in cotton. It was faded, dirty and damp.

I turned and glanced at the crate where the old man had been sitting. Startled, I thought I saw a movement out of the corner of my eye. Looking up at the wooden balcony at the back of the Hall, I screwed up my eyes but there was nothing there. At the bottom of the balcony, was a door. This, I knew, led into the corridor and to some steps which took you up onto the balcony.

'Hey, Chelsea, leave that! He could be up on the balcony or in one of those other rooms. Come on!'

Kicking a pile of papers across the floor, I ran across to the door and pulled it open. Following, Chelsea pushed through behind me, into a shadowy passageway. It smelt of damp and cats. Wooden steps led off to our right, up to the balcony. Beyond the steps the passage was blocked by wood, bricks and slates. A beam of light came down from the hole in the roof above.

Carefully we climbed the steps which turned first to the left onto a small landing and then to the right, up onto the balcony.

The balcony groaned as we stepped onto it. There were still some rows of benches in place and some upturned metal framed chairs with canvas backs and seats. The window at the back was broken. Glass and bricks were scattered down the steps at the back. The balcony was lit by light from the broken window. It was scary like the rooms that boy walked into in that film, *The Sixth Sense*, the one when he could see dead people. But there was no one there. I had to make a noise just to stop the quietness, so I grabbed one of the metal chairs and pushed it over the wooden rail. Chelsea said the rail was called a *balustrade*. There was a lovely crash in the Hall below and I whooped with delight. Trembling and shaking, the balcony was making an awful creaking noise.

'Come on!' shouted Chelsea with panic in her voice. 'Let's get off here! It's dangerous! It could collapse at any time!'

‘Well I don’t care if it does,’ I shouted, running across the balcony and back. It shook and shuddered and creaked. When I got in this mood I wouldn’t listen to anyone. Not even Chelsea.

‘Great! I’m going to make a gang. We’ll let Tom and Adrian and Joe be in it, but first they’ve gotta pass *“**the Test**”*. They’ll have to run across this balcony and back. I bet they won’t do it. Scaredy Cats!’

‘Come away, Craig. Don’t go on it again. It’ll collapse. And you can’t make those others go on it. Besides this is our secret place. We weren’t going to tell anybody else.’

‘Yeh, but you can’t have a ***“gang”*** with only two of us, and you won’t run across. How can I make a flippin’ good test like this, if I don’t have a ***“gang”***?’

I was just about to run across again when we heard a scraping noise coming from down below. We looked over the balcony. We couldn’t see anything. Looking at each other, we crept back down the balcony steps. Quietly and carefully, we edged our way back down the passage.

Standing in the doorway, we both looked into the dark of the main Hall. Sitting very still on the crate and reading a newspaper was the old man. Unable to move, like rabbits in car headlights, we just stood, mouths open, eyes getting wider. Looking at him more carefully now, I could see he was wearing overalls, a white shirt with a green tie and a reddy coloured tweed jacket.

‘It’s him,’ I whispered.

‘Where’s he come from? He wasn’t here before.’

‘From one of them other rooms while we were on the balcony. Come on, I’m for sorting him out.’

Chelsea followed me as we crossed into the middle of the Hall and stood in front of him. I was feeling cocky because Chelsea was there. I could show how big I was. I could show that I was the boss. It was the same feeling I got when I was in class. Once I’d decided I’d had enough, I’d answer the teacher back, tell her to sod off and refuse to do the work. I felt important like a pop star that everyone listened to. Then I felt cocky and nothing could stop me. Nobody could make me do what they wanted. I just went into a rage. It made me feel good. Even though I felt scared inside at the same time.

'Hey, Mister! What're you doing in here? It's our place. You're squattin', you're trespassin'.'

The man looked up at me. He had a big face with flabby cheeks and a double chin. Bits of white hair were combed across his balding head. He smiled in a friendly way.

'I'm the Caretaker.' He spoke quietly, then looked down at his newspaper again.

'You mean you're an old tramp!' I said nastily.

'You've got bad manners, haven't you, Craig?'

'How do you know my flippin' name? Who are you?' I shouted.

'I told you. The Caretaker,' he said simply.

'How can you be the Caretaker?' said Chelsea. 'This place is falling down. Nobody uses it. It doesn't need a Caretaker.'

'It does when you're in here.'

'We can take care of ourselves. Don't need you,' I snapped sulkily.

'Everybody needs a Caretaker. I'm yours.'

'You're mad, you old sod. You better get out of here. This is our place. I'll get the police onto you.'

I could tell Chelsea was beginning to feel sorry for him.

'But what's your name?' she asked.

'Arthur.'

'Arthur, who?'

'Just, Arthur.'

'Well watch this, bloody Arthur.' I bent down and picked up a half brick. Running across the room, I hurled it at a high window pane. There was a crashing sound and pieces of glass fell out onto the floor.

'That'll be you, if you don't scarper.'

'You see,' said Arthur, calmly. 'You do need a Caretaker. You destroy things and you are destroying yourself.'

'I'll destroy things if I want,' I shouted. I knew when I started getting nasty that adults were scared of me. So I picked up another brick, turned round and threw it at the balcony. It bounced off the wooden rail and landed in a pile of rubble on the Hall floor.

'It's you who'll get destroyed if you don't… ' Turning back to face the old man, I was surprised to see that he wasn't there.

'Where'd he go?'

'Dunno. I was watching you. When I looked again, he'd gone.'

'Well, let's find him.'

Shouting threats, I ran all around the building. Into the passage. Onto the balcony. Into all the side rooms. There was no sign of the old man.

'I think we'd better go,' said Chelsea sounding nervous, 'it's getting a bit spooky in here.'

'I bet he won't come back here again,' I said trying to sound big. 'Come on then. Might as well go to the Rec. It's getting boring in here, anyway. And don't tell anybody about him. We'll have everybody coming here, nosing around.'

Three

We were half way through the week. I was back at school. Chelsea had not mentioned Arthur, the Caretaker since Saturday. Neither had I.

But I had remembered the balcony and the idea I'd had for the '***gang Test***'. I thought, if I got Tom, Adrian and Joe to go with me, we could have some fun. If the old man was still there, we could see him off.

At break time, I told them about my idea and about Arthur. I wasn't always that good at keeping secrets.

'Who's this Arthur, then?' asked Tom.

'Well he's a tramp, only not scruffy,' I replied. 'But *he* says he's the Caretaker.'

'How can he be the Caretaker?' interrupted Adrian. 'That place has been shut down for years. My dad says it's an eyesore and should be knocked down. He's having you on. Caretaker? Place is a wreck. There's nothing to caretake. Pull the other leg!'

'I bet you! I bet you! He was there and he said he was the Caretaker,' I said, getting angry.

'What if he's a ghost?' said Joe seriously.

'Ghost? Who-oo-oo- oo! He'll get you if you go in there,' I said mocking Joe, dancing around him and waving my arms.

Winding Joe up was easy and I thought it was great fun. The other two joined in and we danced around Joe, wailing and moaning.

'Get lost! Get lost!' shouted Joe.

'Joe's scared of the Ghost of the Gospel Hall,' I said, laughing.

'No, I'm not! I just said he might be. Ghosts hang about old places like that. It doesn't bother me.'

'Well, let's go ghost hunting after school,' suggested Tom. 'We'll see who's frightened, and who isn't.'

'Yeh, and we can do my ***"gang Test"***. And I bet none of you do it because it's dangerous.'

'I bet you won't do it,' said Adrian.

'Already have done. 'S'easy for me. But, I'll do it again. First. 'Cos I'm the boss. I'll show you lot what to do. Then we'll see who's Scaredy Cats.'

It was Art that afternoon. I like drawing and painting so the time passed quickly, and I didn't get into any trouble. Even when Charlotte Baker said I pinched her paintbrush and snatched it out of my hand, I ignored her and took James Harrison's instead because he never creates a fuss or tells Miss Denton. Besides, I wanted to go home from school with Adrian, Tom and Joe to the Gospel Hall, so I didn't want to be sent home.

As I pushed my way past two girls to get outside at home time, Chelsea grabbed my arm.

'Hey, get off, I'll...' I was shouting with my fists clenched ready to lash out when I realised who it was.

'I heard you saying you were going to the Hall. I thought we said it was our secret place. You've not told those three about Arthur, have you?'

'What if I have? They're my mates. They're not frightened of some old man.'

'You told me not to tell anybody. You said you didn't want anybody nosing around and now you're taking those three...?'

‘We’re only going to do the ***“Test”***. He’s only an old bloke. Probably won’t be there. Now that we’ve seen him in there he’s probably gone somewhere else. Tramps don’t like places if people know they’re there. They don’t like being disturbed.’

‘Well if he’s there don’t hurt him in any way and don’t let those others do anything. He’s only a harmless old man. And be careful in there. It’s not very safe. That balcony could cave in at any time. And it’s a bit...’

‘Spooo- oo- ky! Ohhh!’

‘Hey!’ shouted Adrian from the door. ‘Are you coming Craig, or have you got a date?’

With that, Adrian, Tom and Joe crashed through the doors, laughing and jeering. I pushed several kids out of the way as I chased after them shouting,

‘You little runts! Wait ’til I get you!’

Half way down Rathbone Road, all three stopped to get their breath; laughing at the same time. I caught up with them and grabbed hold of each one in turn around the head, ruffling their hair. ‘Cheeky monkeys!’ I said, ‘bloomin’ Little Hulks. Come on, last one to the Hall is a *Scooby-Doo*!’

Five minutes later we were pushing back the plank from the boarded window and clambering noisily into the darkness.

‘Oh, it’s dark in here,’ said Joe in a quiet, frightened voice.

‘Watch out behind you! It’s a ghost!’ said Adrian, joking.

‘Well, I don’t like it. It’s – it’s...’

‘Spooooky!’ shouted Thomas, in his best howling wolf voice.

‘Shurrup! Come on, your eyes’ll get used to it in a minute,’ I said.

Leading the way, I walked slowly across the Hall with the others following, staring into the darkness and looking around nervously. Adrian stumbled over a large cardboard tube. He picked it up and moaned down it, making a loud 'Oo-oo-oo-oo' echo all around the room. Joe was scared and came and stood close to me. I just laughed.

'Good one, Ade. See this place is full of good things to mess with.'

Picking up another tube which leant against the wall, Tom went into battle against Adrian, cardboard light sabres crashing against each other until Adrian's snapped in the middle and hung down. Quickly I pulled off the bottom half, raised it to my mouth and bellowed down it as loud as I could into Joe's ear. Joe covered his ear and complained, 'That's not funny! You've deafened me, you have!'

Then Adrian did the same to Tom, and Tom swung his tube into my face making a loud trumping noise and banging my nose. The sharp pain made me angry. I pushed the end of the tube into Tom's mouth and he staggered back.

'Wha'd'ya do that for? It was only a bit of fun.'

'Yeh, but it hurt my bloomin' nose!' I shouted angrily. Once again I felt the anger rise in me. I felt I had to hurt someone because I was hurt.

But then Adrian calmed us down.

'Hey, you two, I thought we were gonna do some ***"gang Test"***?'

'And where's that man you were on about?' asked Joe.

'Dunno, dunno,' I said. 'He isn't always here. Bet he's found somewhere else since I told him to get out. Come on, let's go to the balcony.'

Four

Standing at the top of the stairs, on the edge of the balcony, my three friends did not look impressed.

'Yeh, a balcony. So what?' said Tom.

'What kind of ***"Test"*** are you gonna make of that? Do we flippin' well have to jump off?' mocked Adrian.

'It doesn't look safe to me,' said Joe.

'Got it in one, Joe. Look, I'll show you.'

I ran across the balcony. It groaned and shook. Adrian, Tom and Joe took a step backwards towards the stairs.

From the other side I shouted, 'It can go at any time. But I don't care. Doesn't bother me. Watch!'

I bounded back across the balcony. It creaked and shuddered. There was a low, grating noise and something fell, crashing and smashing in the Hall below.

''S'easy! Across and back. Let's see who passes the ***"Test"***. Let's see who's a Scaredy Cat!'

'Joe's right. It's not very safe. It could give way at any time,' murmured Tom.

'That's the point! It can only be a proper ***"gang Test"*** if it's dangerous,' I said.

'Well, I'll go next,' volunteered Adrian. 'These two softies can watch like girls.'

Adrian walked out onto the balcony. It swayed and creaked. Adrian stood still. He looked back at us. His face was serious and white. Then, clenching his fists, he ran as fast as he could to the far side. The balcony seemed to sink and move. There was a loud tearing, cracking noise. Adrian turned round. He was stranded at the other side. His face seemed even whiter.

I shouted to him. 'You've got to come back or else you've not done the ***"Test"***. Anyway, you can't stay there all night.'

Adrian bit his bottom lip in the way he always did in lessons when he was concentrating. Then, in a sudden movement, he ran fast across the balcony and crashed into us with one last desperate lunge. It was like the grinding sound in the film, *Titanic,* when the ship went up into the air on its end then slowly sank into the sea. Adrian was breathing hard but he tried to stop it and appear all right. He gave me a high-five and we whooped like those people in the audience on telly when somebody famous comes on.

''S-a doddle. Nowt to it, if you've got the nerve.' Adrian was laughing now and showing off. 'Reckon you did it first, Craig, so you should be ***"Gang Leader"*** and I should be next. C'mon you two, who's going next? Not weeing ourselves, are we?' Adrian was acting big, but I could see him still trembling. I knew he'd been scared.

'Better be me,' said Tom. But he didn't sound very sure.

Tom looked across the balcony and hesitated. I gave him a big push. He went flying, but didn't fall, raced across, planted his feet on the opposite wall, pushed off and sprinted back across. There was a lot of shaking, but it was as if the balcony was taken by surprise. Nothing gave way.

Tom high-fived Adrian and me and we all danced round Joe.

'C'mon Joe! Your turn! Joe, Joe, Joe!' I began chanting. Then the other two joined in. 'Joe, Joe, Joe, Joe…'

He seemed frozen solid. I noticed the wetness in his eyes.

'Hey, look! Joe's crying! Joe's a softy!'

A tear rolled down one cheek, then another and another. Within seconds he was sobbing. It was like he couldn't get his breath.

'Blood – bloody – bal – balcony!' He was sniffling. 'What's – good – about – it? Running across… What for?'

'C'mon Joe! It's not that bad. You can do it,' said Tom.

''S'easy!' said Adrian. 'Just go as fast as you can. It'll be OK.'

'But – but –' He was crying out loud now. 'But – but – you've – made – it – weaker – it's gonna – gonna – fall. I'm not – not – doin' it! I'm not!'

'Well if you don't do it, you can't be in the gang.' I was the leader and I couldn't let him off.

'Don't care! Don't care! Don't want – want to be – in the gang!'

He was annoying me with his crying. I felt the anger in me rising.

'And anyone who doesn't do it gets the punishment. We'll put you in the middle of the balcony, and jump up and down on it.'

'No! You can't! I'm going home!' The three of us moved towards him. Adrian and me each grabbed an arm,

'No – no – don't!' Joe was getting hysterical. 'I'll – I'll – try – honest – give me – some time – I'll …'

We dragged Joe forward. He was struggling and screaming and shouting. He pulled his arm backwards and his elbow hit me on my cheekbone. The pain made me really angry. I pulled on his arm and flung him forward.

Joe went sprawling onto the balcony and landed in the middle on his knees. The balcony shuddered and sank. Joe howled. There was a loud tearing noise. Joe clung onto a bench and didn't move a muscle. The balcony moved again and then stopped. It was definitely sagging in the middle. Like one of those ugly stone creature statues on churches, Joe knelt, very still, not daring to move.

'Get up, Joe!' shouted Tom. 'The faster you go the better. Hurry up! Or it'll give way on you!' Tom sounded frightened.

It didn't bother me. I only laughed and shouted, 'It's gonna go! It's gonna go! Joe, Joe, you're gonna go!'

'I can't move. It'll go if I do.' There was a loud creaking sound and the balcony jerked again.

'Help! Help! It's gonna fall… It's…'

Suddenly there was a strong smell of pipe smoke. A voice from behind made us jump,

'Don't worry, son! Don't move! I'll get you! You'll be all right. Don't move!'

In one movement we all turned round. It was Arthur, the Caretaker. Stepping between us, he moved forward silently and smoothly. He walked out, almost floated out onto the balcony. It did not move. Not even the smallest tremble. Reaching out, he appeared to grab Joe's hand and then Joe was sent through the air, crashing into us. We grabbed hold of him. None of us quite saw what happened next, but there was a terrific rumble, like the loudest thunder and a scraping sound. We looked across to see the wooden floorboards, benches, chairs, all caving in. It was as if they were being sucked into a big hole. I couldn't see Arthur. He had disappeared into the hole. There was crashing and crunching and smashing. Dust went up into the air in a big cloud. Coughing and spluttering, we quickly jumped down the stairs into the corridor.

'Blood and sand!' I shouted, saying what my mum always said when she was angry or shocked by something. Like when we came home and somebody had broken in and had stolen the DVD player, she just stood there and said, *'Blood and Sand!'*

'We've had it now! That poor man – let's gerrout of here fast,' said Tom.

‘I told you! I told you! You wouldn’t bloody listen!’ Joe was still crying and moaning.

I ran, first, into the main hall. The broken wood was piled high with mortar and bricks and rubble was scattered everywhere. It was like in the news on telly which showed all the mess after the big wave had destroyed all the people’s houses and killed thousands in that country. Clouds of dust filled the hall and stayed in the air, some dropping down onto my hair. I put my hand over my mouth to stop the dust getting in. There was no sign of the Caretaker. He must have been buried under all the rubble.

‘Whattabout that man?’ said Tom, coughing and choking. ‘Where is he?’

‘Under there! Serves him right for being in here when it’s our place.’

‘But he saved Joe,’ said Adrian.

‘So, what! It’s his own bloomin’ lookout,’ I said.

‘Bloomin’ hell! He’s under there – he’s – he’s –’

‘Bloomin’dead!’ I said in my cockiest, hardest voice.

‘Let’s get outta here! C’mon! I’m going!’ shouted Tom.

‘Police’ll – they’ll get us – get us – for this –’ Joe was still sobbing.

‘Nowt to do with me. We didn’t do anythin’. I’m outta here,’ said Adrian. Then he ran across the hall and snatched open the plank. The other two followed and they all climbed out into the sunlight. I stood and looked at the pile and watched the dust settling, and then I followed on.

Five

It was Thursday morning. We were in class waiting for registration before we went to assembly. Me, Tom and Adrian were talking about our ***'gang Test'*** in the Hall. Joe hadn't arrived at school. Adrian said he'd called for Joe, but his mum said he wasn't well. In fact his mother phoned school later to say that he felt sick and had a headache so he couldn't come in.

'We know what's wrong with him, lads, don't we?' I said to Tom and Adrian. 'Great, wasn't it? Whattacrash! Better than breaking anything! Went with a bang! Dust and bricks and wood an' everything flying everywhere. Like one of them car bombs you see on the news in that place. Ka-boom!'

'You mean Iraq. And did you see it nearly go when I went across,' said Adrian.

'Well, I was after you,' said Tom. 'An' I had to go real fast before it went. Did you see it? I went so quickly, it hardly shook. I bet I was fastest.'

'But you lot have only done it once. I did it loads. And besides, it's scarier when you go slow, like Joe…'

'We shouldn't be going on like this. We're forgettin' that old man. Whattabout him? We'd better not tell anybody else.'

'Nobody'll know. And what if somebody finds out. They don't know we've been in there,' I said.

'Do you think he's – he's –' started Tom. He looked pale and worried.

'Dead? Well, he was under all that wood and rubble. Bound to be,' I said.

'But whattabout Joe? He knows, an' he's a right *"soft boy"*. He might say something,' Adrian said suddenly.

I smiled one of my nasty grins.

'Don't worry about Joey boy. I rang him last night on the mobile, and I told him what would happen if he told anybody. An' when he comes back to school we'll give him a little reminder.'

It always makes me grin when I think how I can hurt somebody, or how I can get my own back on teachers when they try to make me do something I don't like. Or when they stop me from doing something, like texting on my phone. Just because they say it's against school rules. I can do it at home, so why can't I do it at school? So, I just refuse and carry on and then they get nasty and want to get my phone off me. I say, *'It's mine, you can't have it!'* They can't touch me. I'll get them done if they do.

Then Miss Denton asked Adrian and Tom to give out some books.

I said, 'Hey, we were talking. They don't have to do your jobs. They're not your slaves. Don't do it lads. Let her do it herself.'

'Now that's enough, Craig. Don't start the day off badly.'

Adrian and Tom carried on giving out books so then I said, 'Miss, can I help them?'

'Only if you don't think you're being forced into slavery, Craig.'

I laughed, 'OK Miss, I'll give 'em a hand.' So I ran across to Adrian and snatched half of the books out of his hands.

Then she said, 'Right everybody, sit down and get ready for registration.' She didn't lose her temper or shout at me really badly or tried to make me leave the room because she knew I wouldn't. She knew I'd kick up a big fuss. I like it when I know teachers are scared of me. If anybody else had said that, they'd have been sent to Mr Dawson straight away.

I finished giving out the books and went and sat next to Chelsea. I was just going to make some of my funny noises because I didn't like that daft register calling business where you had to answer 'Here Miss' or 'Good morning Miss', then Chelsea said, 'Did you go to the Hall?'

'Yep,' I said. 'It was great. We did my ***"Test"***. On the balcony. Me and Tom and Adrian all did it…'

Miss had started calling the register.

'…but Joe was a real chicken. An' guess what? He was right in the middle an' it began to collapse – '

'Oh, no! I told you it was dangerous. You shouldn't have gone on it. Is Joe all right?'

'Course he is. 'Cos guess what? And you'd better keep this a secret…'

'I will.'

'By the Sword of The Sorcerer!' I'd seen this on a cartoon where the hero made all his followers stick with him and do as he said. And when he did he always shouted, "By the Sword of The Sorcerer!"

'Yes. By the Sword of The Sorcerer!'

'You'd better!' Then I said in my best nasty, cruel voice, 'Or your throat will be slit and your tongue cut out.'

'What happened Craig?'

'He came. That stupid old tramp, Caretaker, whatever, appeared on the balcony and went out and shoved Joe back to us and then – then the balcony went. Like an earthquake. You should have heard the noise. Deafening. The whole place shook. Dust and wood and bricks everywhere…'

'But, what about Arthur?'

'Dunno! Didn't see. He must have been buried under a ton of rubble.'

'But, Craig, he must be hurt or– or– '

'It's his own daft fault. Not ours. He shouldn't have been in there. And you'd better not tell anybody.'

'I won't, but, didn't you go and see if he was all right?'

'Now, Chelsea,' said Miss Denton in a loud voice. 'Don't you think you should stop talking and be ready for assembly?'

Going down to the assembly hall, Adrian and Tom were next to me in the line. Chelsea wanted to get next to me to go on in my ear about the Caretaker but Miss made her open doors for everyone. But it was just as bad with those two because they kept going on about the old man. They said what if someone had heard the noise and went to look. That really worried me too at the time, but it happened, and that was yesterday. And, I wasn't bothered any more. Besides nobody'd come running to see and there'd been no police cars or anything like that. If they had come running, all that they would have seen was a big pile of rubble. I told them this but they still looked scared and kept going on. In the end I shouted, 'Shurrup, will yer!'

Miss Denton stopped the line and told me off. 'Craig, where do you think you are? We go into assembly in silence, not shouting.'

'Well, they're bugging me. Won't shut up with their stupid little voices.' I elbowed Adrian in the stomach and punched Tom in the back.

Miss was angry. 'I did not ask for an answer! Your behaviour is disgraceful! There can be no excuse for shouting and punching people. You're in Year 5 and a Reception child could show you how to behave.'

'So, what!' I said in my worst, snarly voice.

She pulled me out of the line, saying, in an angry voice, 'You will sit out of assembly and then see me at playtime.'

'Get off! Get off my arm! You're hurting me! Leave me alone! I'll get you done,' I shouted, and, twisting round, I threw myself onto the corridor floor and sat by the wall.

'You'll just have to sit there by yourself. I am reporting this to Mr Dawson.'

'Please yourself! Don't care!' I said in a sulk.

Mr Dawson is the head teacher and he is bald with a moustache and spit comes out of his mouth when he gets angry and tells you off. He wears glasses and I'm nearly as tall as him.

I was trembling inside, because I was so angry at being blamed for telling them two to be quiet. I was calming down as Miss led the line into assembly. Jacob Jackson turned round and pointed at me and laughed. I couldn't let him get away with that. I hated him and the anger came up into my chest again. I jumped up, gave him a kick and then fell down against the wall again.

Miss didn't see. And Jacob went along holding his bottom and moaning and groaning. That was funny. It made me snigger to myself. Serves him right. Nobody laughs at me and gets away with it.

As I calmed down I was annoyed with myself. I hadn't wanted to get into trouble. I'd wanted to go into assembly. It wasn't fair. I'd got done for nothing. When people told me off, nagged me, I couldn't stand it. I always had to show them.

I crept down the corridor and sat outside the yellow double doors of the assembly hall. It was a very big hall and we did PE and Assembly in there, and had our dinners in there too. They'd just finished singing a hymn, *"Everybody's Building"*. I was a bit peeved because I liked that one because you could do actions to pretend you were building and nobody would tell you off. I hated, *"Give me Oil in Your Lamp"*. I've never seen a lamp using oil. You always just flick a switch and it comes on. It's a load of rubbish, doesn't make sense, does silly, *"Give me Oil in Your Lamp"*.

Then Mr Dawson did his story. He always does a story. It's usually a story that is about nowadays or about somebody famous who's done good things, but in the end he always talks about Jesus or The Bible. I sat up closer to the door when he said, 'Do you know any old people? Your gran or granddad or someone who lives in your street, or who you see at the supermarket?' I could see through one of the thin glass panels in the door. Hands shot up everywhere.

'Have you talked to them, helped them? Or do you think they're just old people and not worth bothering about? This morning I'm going to tell you about an old man who was badly treated because some children thought he was old and useless…'

The breath stopped in my throat. My heart was beating fast and the backs of my hands were pricking. Did he know? Had someone reported it? Had somebody seen us and phoned him and said they saw some boys from our school? I strained my neck to try and see Adrian or Tom or Chelsea to see what they were doing. But they couldn't have seen the old man and what happened. I was beginning to panic and that's when I run off sometimes. What if they'd heard the crash and gone in and found that old Caretaker under the rubble?

'…and a lonely old lady who was helped by a young boy… A *Good Samaritan.* You know, one day I'll be old, some of you might think I am now…' Some of the teachers sitting round the side of the hall laughed politely, '…And all of you will one day be old, and old people can be sometimes lonely. Can anyone think of any little acts of kindness we could do to help older people feel happy and wanted?'

Once again I could see hands shooting up.

'Help them with their shopping.'

'Yes. Good.'

'Help them cross the road. '

'Well done. Another good idea.'

'Perhaps talk to them, because the old man in our road always stands, leaning on the gate, and I sometimes say "Hello" to him.'

'Excellent. All good answers.'

Then Mr Dawson started to tell us a story about an old man who had a conker tree in his back garden and some children got over the fence to throw things up at the conkers. He explained how the old man had come out to see what the noise was, and the gang threw conkers at him. He stumbled and fell over. I thought that was funny; peppering him with conkers, just like snowballing. Anyway, in the story, the children ran away. The old man was hurt and he couldn't get up. He lay there for an hour until a neighbour saw him and phoned for an ambulance.

I breathed a sigh of relief because it was nothing to do with our old Caretaker and, as I did so, my arm slipped and I fell against the door. The nearest teacher, Mr Blake, saw me through the glass panel but he ignored me because he was used to me not being in assembly and I bet he didn't want to interrupt Mr Dawson's story.

The other story was about an old lady who had gone to the shops and left her key in the back door, and when she got back, she was locked out. She was crying and then a boy who lived up the road, came past, and he went and got his dad's ladder and climbed in through an open bedroom window. Then the boy let the old lady in. She was so happy she gave him a big piece of cake.

'Who was right and who was wrong? Who was the Good Samaritan? Listen and I'll tell you about the *Good Samaritan*. Then you can judge for yourself.'

I knew who it was. We all knew who it was, but we had to hear about Jesus and one of his stories in The Bible. After that Mr Dawson said, 'Let us pray. Put your hands together and close your eyes.'

I never liked the prayer bit. Talking to God, Mr Dawson called it. Why should we have to talk to God? He never talks to us. My mum says it's all rubbish. She says there's no such thing as God. Just people. And if you don't watch out for yourself, no one else will. So, I never liked prayers. I slid on my bottom down the three steps leading to the hall doors and then walked back along the corridor, jumping up at Miss James's hanging mobiles outside her classroom and batting them hard with my hand. At the end of the corridor I looked back and smiled. All the mobiles were waving about like there was a wind down the corridor. It was great.

Six

When everybody came back in class, I was using a plastic ruler to flick screwed up bits of paper across the desk. The first lesson was Literacy and I never usually liked that because I couldn't be bothered reading. Some of the words were too hard for me. And I hated writing because it took me ages to write one sentence. Why do we have to spell words in a certain way? Why can't you write them down like they sound, like I do? I was just going to flick some paper with a ruler at the back of Adrian's head when Miss Denton said:

'Today we are going to follow up Mr Dawson's assembly. In our Literacy lesson we're going to talk about old people – what they look like, the things they do, their habits. Our target is to write a description or poem about an old person. Then, later, we're going to draw and colour portraits of old people.'

Old people. Drawing. I stopped fiddling. I like drawing. I shot my hand up.

'Yes, Craig.'

'Can we use felt tip pens when we do the drawings?'

'Well, we're not doing Art now. That'll be later. We're going to write poems and descriptions first. But, yes, when we come to the portraits you can use felt tips, colouring pencils, wax crayons, paint.'

'Yab-a-dab-a-doo!' I shouted in an excited squeaky voice. Everyone laughed. Even Miss smiled. I liked it when I did or said anything funny and everybody laughed and looked at me.

Then Miss said, 'Now let's start with our *Shared Time*. Everyone very quietly come and sit round me on the carpet.'

We all sat down. I was sitting right behind Jacob Jackson. I couldn't stop myself from slyly pinching his bottom. He made a noise, turned round and frowned at me. He said, 'You'd better watch it, Hartshorn. I'll tell my big brother and he'll do you over.'

I made a funny face back and said, 'Boo-hoo! I'm dead worried now.'

Miss looked at both of us. I was smiling. Jacob was scowling.

'Jacob, I think you'd better come and sit here. Right by my feet where you can concentrate.' Jacob got up. He was angry.

'It was him, Miss. He pinched me and he kicked me when we was in the line going into assembly.'

'I didn't!' I shouted. I hated it when someone told on me, so I never said the truth because they shouldn't try and get me in trouble.

'Wait 'til our Chris gets hold of you. He'll mangle you!'

'Come here, Jacob. That's enough from the pair of you. We're here to work. I am not listening to things which happened earlier. We need to get started.'

Miss read us some descriptions from books about old people and some poems as well. She read us the bits from *Charlie and The Chocolate Factory*, about Grandpa Joe and Grandma Josephine. She also read us a description of the old miser from that *Scrooge* story. I liked watching that on telly at Christmas. About all them ghosts coming to see him at Christmas, and he changes and becomes a nice man. But best of all I liked the poem about *Billy Medals* who was old and sat there thinking about when he was in the war.

Then we talked about old people we knew, what they looked like and what kind of things they did. Miss Denton also asked for some good describing words.

Chelsea put her hand up and said:

'Wrinkled and wizard' or something that sounded like that. Miss said these were excellent words and wrote them on the whiteboard. She's like that, is Chelsea. Good at everything. Wish I knew good words and could read and write like Chelsea.

I looked round at Adrian and Tom and Chelsea and then put my hand up.

'Miss, I knew an old man who lived near me. He always wore a jacket and overall…' I looked across at the others. They looked very nervous and scared. So I was enjoying myself. '…And he had a bald head and big cheeks and he was always smoking a pipe and reading a newspaper.'

'Very good, Craig. You could write that into a description or even make a poem. You see, just like that example, some of the best writing is based on our experiences, people and places we know. You can have a team point for that, Craig.'

Miss Denton always gave me team points or stickers if I did any little bit of work or helped tidying up. She was always trying to make me be good by giving me rewards. If Chelsea had said it, she wouldn't have given her a team point. When I was in a good mood it made me feel good, but sometimes I couldn't care less about silly team points and stickers. Lots of kids did good things for them but it was like treating you like babies. I knew better. I'd get points if I wanted them, but they wouldn't make me do what they wanted.

We all went back to our tables to write about old people. I was sitting next to Chelsea so that she could help me with words. As we were working, there was a quick knock on the door. Mr Dawson came in.

'Everyone working hard I see, Miss Denton. Has everyone been listening well and trying their best?' Mr Dawson looked straight at me. 'Nobody has been misbehaving or disrupting the class?'

I knew he was coming to check up on me. I felt like throwing my pencil across the room, getting up and running out. I knew it was because I'd not gone into assembly. But that was before and he shouldn't be coming to see if I was being good now. That had gone. Teachers always go on about things you've done before. My mum, when she got fed up of me getting into trouble, said I got the blame because I was always being bad. She said it was *"Give a dog a bad name"*. But I'm not a dog, and my name's Craig. Anyway, I just bit the end of my pencil and kicked the chair underneath the table instead.

'No, Mr Dawson. Everyone has done really well.'

'Ah, good. Thank you.' Mr Dawson turned and went back out.

With Chelsea's help with words, I managed to write a good poem about *"The Old Man"*. Chelsea finished her own description then she said to me:

'Craig, don't you think you'd better check up on Arthur to see what happened to him? To see if he's all right? You can't just leave him there. It's not right.'

To Chelsea things were either right or wrong and she didn't like doing anything wrong. She never got in bother in school and somehow, even if I could, I never wanted to get her into any trouble.

'But what do we do when we find his body. We can't tell anybody. We'd be in dead trouble.'

'No, you wouldn't. You didn't push him off or anything. It was a dangerous place to be but it was an accident. Nobody's going to blame you. In fact you could be quite a hero; the boy who discovered the plight of the old man…'

'People don't believe me! The teachers won't! The cops won't! My mum won't! They'll just say, it's that bad Craig. He did it!'

'But that's not true! You didn't do it! But if somebody finds him and they know you've been there, then they might wonder why you didn't tell anybody, especially about a balcony collapsing on an old man.'

'Old tramp, more like! Living in there! Nobody'll miss him! Nobody'll know any different!'

'But you will know, Craig! Couldn't you – couldn't we – just go and have a look…?' Chelsea knew what to say to me next, '…Or are you too scared, too chicken…?'

'You what! Me chicken! Doesn't bother me!'

Chelsea didn't say anything more. She knew I'd think about being chicken. She knew that I'd have to show her that I wasn't scared of anything or anybody.

'Anyway,' she said, 'let's read through your poem and see how it sounds.'

This was my poem:

The Old Man

I know an old man
who lives in an old hall.
He's bald with a few white
hairs on his head and all.
He has fat cheeks,
he wears a jacket
and a white shirt and overalls.
He sits on a milk crate
and reads his paper till late.

By Craig

I took my poem to Miss Denton and she read it out to the class and gave me two team points and a *'Good Work'* sticker on the bottom. I'd done enough writing and sitting and I felt fidgety. I couldn't sit down much longer. I needed to be moving about. It was like my arms and legs were tingling and I had to move them. So I said to Miss, 'Can I go and show it to Mr Hughes and Mrs Flint, please?' I said it in my best polite voice. My mum had said once to Mr Dawson that, at home, I could be the most polite boy. But I only liked being polite when I wanted something. I liked it when everybody fussed me and I'd done something good. That's when I feel I should be able to do what I want, so I would use my polite voice. And now I just wanted to go for a walk around, because I hated being in the same place for a long time. Unless I was on my *PlayStation*.

'Well, you've worked hard, Craig, and that is a good poem. I'm sure Mr Hughes and Mrs Flint will be pleased to read it.' I knew Miss would let me go because she thought I might do more good work if everyone praised me. But I really wanted to go and mess around, so I said, 'Can Adrian come with me?'

'No, Craig. I don't think you need an escort. I think you can find your way very well by yourself. Besides Adrian has not finished his work yet. Off you go! It'll soon be playtime.'

As I went out of the door Miss was busy going round marking work and talking about good ideas for writing. So I nodded to Adrian and mouthed to him to ask Miss if he could go to the toilet. With five fingers up I was telling him to wait five minutes. Then I went out and waited behind the yellow fire doors at the end of the corridor. After five minutes Adrian came out through the doors.

'We'll nip to Mr Hughes and then Mrs Flint and then we'll go for a mess around in the toilets,' I said.

'I thought Mr Dawson knew about the old man in assembly. I wasn't half wetting myself,' said Adrian.

'Don't fuss yourself! Nobody knows about it. It'd have been on the news. Everybody'd 'ave been goin' on about it. Anyway I'm going in there after school to see what happened. Are you coming?'

'Are you a nutter, Craig? What'ya gonna do if you find his body?'

'Dunno yet. Are you coming?'

'Er… Well, I've got to go and see – and see my cousin straight after school, with my mum and dad.'

'I'll tell you what I find tomorrow. You go and hide in the small cloakroom and I'll nip in with this.'

I went in to both teachers and got more team points and stickers. Then Adrian and me went into the toilets. I turned all the sink taps on and they were splashing everywhere.

'I know,' I shouted to Adrian, laughing, 'let's make some plugs for the sinks.' We couldn't have plugs because kids would leave them in and flood the place. After the last time that the toilet floor was flooded, Mr Forbes, the caretaker, had removed all the plugs. So we made plugs out of screwed up paper towels, stuck one in every plug hole and turned all the taps on. Then I made a wet paper towel bomb and threw it at the back of Adrian's neck. The water ran down his neck and he jumped about like one of them puppets on a string, screaming like a piggy-wig. I couldn't stop laughing. Adrian made one and threw it at me. I dodged and it splattered on the wall and stuck there. We both laughed out loud. Then I threw another soggy paper towel up in the air and it stuck on the ceiling. Suddenly the water was spilling out of the sinks and splashing on to the tiles. Quickly we both turned off the taps.

'Hey, come on Adrian! We'd better tell Miss Denton about this mess.'

We both dashed into the classroom out of breath, banging the door behind us and shouting, 'Miss! Miss! There's a mess…'

Miss Denton was just reading out someone's poem.

'What on earth are you doing? Barging into the classroom and shouting out. How very rude you are!'

'But, Miss,' I said, 'somebody's flooded the toilets.'

'There's water all over the floor,' added Adrian.

'Wait! Calm down! Why have you been into the toilets, Craig?'

'I was bursting for a wee!' Everyone laughed. Miss had asked for that one.

'Stop – being – so – rude!' She said in her slowest, nastiest voice. She was getting annoyed. 'Now tell me – one at a time – what has happened. Craig.'

'Well, Miss, I went to Mr Hughes and Mrs Flint and then I needed the toilet. As I was going in Adrian came running out. He nearly knocked me over. He said, "Look in here. Have you seen this mess? We'd better tell Miss." And, Miss, some naughty kid has stuffed paper towels in the plug holes and left the taps running. We turned off the taps and took the paper towels out and came to tell you.'

Some girls made a silly "a-r-r-w" noise and some boys laughed and everybody started chattering.

'Stop all this noise at once!' Miss Denton said to the class. 'Is it very wet?'

'You can paddle in there, Miss,' said Adrian.

'Shall I go and tell Mr Forbes, Miss?'

'I think you better had. And well done for acting so quickly and sensibly.'

I beckoned to Adrian and went running to the door but Miss said, 'You go by yourself Craig. Adrian come and sit down. You've got work to finish.'

So I ran down and told Mr Forbes and then walked very slowly back to class.

Adrian and me got a team point each. That meant I'd got six team points already. The rest of the day went quite well. I only got into one fight at dinnertime and in the dining hall the dinner lady praised me for eating all my dinner and gave me a sticker.

In the afternoon we did the old people portraits. Miss showed us how to draw different types of face shapes and how to draw lines across the face to put the eyes, nose and mouth in the right places. She showed us how to make faces look old by putting wrinkles around the eyes and lines round the mouth and on the lips. I liked the little red lines on the eyeballs which were to show veins. I drew a really good one and Miss Denton said she was going to put it on backing paper and put it up on the wall.

'Hey, Tom!' I said as we were lining up at home time, 'I'm going to the Gospel Hall – have a look what happened to that old tramp. Are you coming?'

'Er – well – I would – but I've got to go to football training as soon as we get out.'

'Yer a pair of chickens, you and Adrian. Just as bad as Joe. Scared of what yer'll find.'

'Well he might be – might be – '

'Dead! Probably is. Won't bother me though. I'll just bury him again. I suppose you and Adrian are only youngsters. You're not even ten yet. I've been ten for ages, you little Baby Bunkins!' I was feeling big and important on the outside. But inside, I was feeling a bit nervous and scared. I'd never seen a dead body before except for a bird I found in the back garden and it had all white wriggly maggots inside it. I just kicked it under the bushes.

Standing in the line waiting to file out to go home, a hand tugged at my elbow. It was Chelsea. We dropped back to the end of the line.

'We're still going aren't we?'

'Yeh. Course.'

'I'll call for you after tea.'

Seven

I was stuffing burger into my mouth and taking big swigs from a can of Coke whilst drop kicking *'The Animal'* on '*Wrestle 2000'* on my *PlayStation.*

'Did you say you got three team points and stickers, Craig?' asked my mum.

'Doh!' I said with bits of bun flying out of my mouth. 'Doh! Flippin' thix,' I said stuffing some more food in.

'What? Don't speak when your mouth's full!'

I swallowed quickly and wiped some tomato sauce from my mouth. I was narked.

'I said flippin' well six team points and I got three stickers. I did a brilliant poem and Miss Denton said my picture was the best one and it was going up on the wall.'

'That's good, Craig, but it's no use if you get in bother tomorrow. You'd better not get sent home because I've got to go on business to town tomorrow. So think on, or else I'll ground you and you won't see that *PlayStation* for a long time.'

'But I've been good! I bet I was best in the class!' I shouted.

'Well, make sure you keep it that way. Or else! Anyway, listen. I've got to nip over to Mary's now. Will you be all right for an hour or so?'

'Chelsea's calling for me in a mo. We're going out playing.'

‘Well, make sure you take your key and don’t be out too long. See you later, love. Get yourself some pop and crisps after.’

‘Can Chelsea come in and have some?’

‘If she doesn’t stay too long. I don’t want her mother coming round here looking for her when I’m not in.’

‘She won’t. She’s sensible is Chelsea. She knows when to go home.’

‘That’s true. Wish you were more like that. Sometimes wonder why she mates around with you. She never gets in any bother at school. Anyway, are you sure you’ll be OK? I’m going now.’

‘Course. I’m not a little *baby*. Besides I’ve got Mary’s number on my mobile.’

‘Bye love.’

I knew mum was going drinking again with Mary. I knew she wouldn’t be back in an hour. More like eleven o’clock or something like that. But it didn’t bother me. It meant I could do what I wanted. As long as I was in my bedroom and I didn’t make any mess.

Ten minutes later Chelsea knocked on the door and we went off down the street heading for the Gospel Hall.

‘I’m scared,’ said Chelsea. ‘What if we find him all…?’

‘Crushed and mangled with blood all over him and his brains hanging out…’

‘Don’t Craig! It’s not funny. That poor old man. I don’t know what we’ll do if he’s – he’s – ’

‘Well you wanted to go. We could have just left it.’

‘I know. But we can’t just leave him.’

‘C’mon, let’s get on with it,’ I said cockily. But deep down, I didn’t want to find a dead body.

My hand was shaking when I began to pull back the plank, so I turned myself towards it so that Chelsea couldn’t see. Pulling the plank too far I accidentally let it go and it banged shut across the opening. I jumped and just managed to stop myself from shouting out loud.

I clambered through and shone my torch into the gloom. I didn't usually take a torch but somehow, this time, it felt better with a torch. Like it was some kind of weapon which would protect me. As I stood up and Chelsea was just climbing through the gap, there was a sudden swoosh right in front of me. This time an electric shock went through my arms and hands and the hairs on the back of my neck seemed to prickle. I couldn't help shouting out this time as I stepped back nearly knocking Chelsea over.

'What was that?' asked Chelsea sounding really scared.

Even as she was saying this I saw the pigeon swoop up to a place high in the beams.

'A pigeon! A flippin' pigeon! Very near hit me in the bloomin' face.' I was feeling angry now and this helped me not to feel so scared.

I shone the torch and moved the beam across the far balcony end. The platform at the top of the steps which led to the balcony was still there. Then there was a gaping blackness where the balcony should have been. And instead, twisted wooden railings hung down and plaster and brick had been ripped from the walls.

I put the torch beam on the pile of rubble. It was a big pile with bricks and plaster and wood and benches and chairs.

'Wow!' said Chelsea. 'What a mess! He couldn't possibly have survived that lot.'

'C'mon. Let's go and look.'

'We might have to tell somebody. It'll need lots of men or a digger to clear that lot.'

'Well if he's under there, nobody'll find him, so it'll be no trouble to us. No point in telling anybody.'

'But what about his relatives? They'll miss him and tell the police. They need to know, Craig.'

'But he was a tramp. Squatting in here. He'll have no relatives. Even if he has, they won't care. And we don't know who they are. C'mon.'

I was feeling brave now. I took big strides down to the pile of rubble. Chelsea followed about a couple of metres behind me. She was taking small steps. She didn't want to go.

I scrambled up the pile and stood on top of it.

'I'm the King of the castle. You're a dirty rascal,' I shouted.

'Craig! Shush! Somebody will hear you,' said Chelsea, moving closer.

So then I started throwing pieces of wood and bricks and chunks of mortar off the pile.

'C'mon! Help me! Let's see if there's any sign…'

Chelsea came closer. I got a piece of wooden rail and started to push bricks and rubble off the heap. But it was hard going and I wasn't really getting into the pile.

'Why are you doing that?'

I was going to shout back at Chelsea, 'You know why!' but I realised it wasn't her voice. In fact it was a man's voice.

Alarmed, we both turned round at the same time. In front of us, in the middle of the Hall, was the old man, Arthur. He was sucking on a pipe and looking straight at us.

'What are you doing lad?'

For a moment I couldn't speak. My mouth opened and closed, but no words came out. I couldn't believe my eyes.

'You? How could – I saw you – the balcony went – in the middle. You were still on it – you should be – how? – how?– '

'Light on my feet, lad. Like a cat.'

'You couldn't. You're too…'

'Old? Older than you think, lad. But sometimes us olduns know more than you youngsters. We know a life where we're like acrobats, eagles soaring on wings, defying gravity, defying the laws of the world. You're only young. Think you know all the answers. But, there's a lot more to be learnt out there.'

'Didn't you get hurt at all, Arthur?' asked Chelsea.

'Not a scratch, my love. Must be someone up there looking out for me.'

'We thought you were buried. You should be dead!'

'And I might have been, and perhaps I am. But it would have been because of you. So, you should be happy.'

'Happy? What's it to me? Better if you were under that rubble. Now you're still trespassing in our place.'

'He's right, Craig. He's here. He's not under the rubble. You should be glad.'

'Well, I'm not!'

'What are you scared of?' said Arthur.

'Nothing! Nothing scares me! Nothing! And nobody!'

'But you are. Everything you do and say tells me you're scared. You get angry at school because you are scared. You break things and hurt people because you are scared. You shout at me because you are scared.'

'I'm not! I'm not! Stop saying that you silly old...'

'Craig. You've got to face things. You're scared of yourself. You think you can't do things at school. Instead of trying, you do what you think you're good at: refusing to do things, screaming, shouting, hurting others, destroying, trying to get expelled because you're scared you can't do your work. You're scared nobody likes you. But when you stop running scared, look what you do. A great poem. Wonderful drawing of me.'

'How do you know that? Who told you that? Was it you Chelsea?'

'This is the first time I've seen Arthur since I was last here with you. I've never been here by myself. Do you really think I'd tell other people about school?'

'Then it must have been that little rat Adrian or…'

‘No, Craig! Nobody! I just know. I am a Caretaker. Caretakers can take care of people as well as places. I’m here to take care of you. To help you with your anger and fears. If you like, I’m a Scaretaker.’

I was really angry now. Tears were beginning to run down my cheeks. I held my fists tight and began to beat them together. Nobody’d ever told me I was scared before. Teachers, Learning Mentors who came to my home, my mum, other kids, nobody!

‘You just shut up! I’m not scared! I’ll show you! I’ll bloomin’ well do for you!’

I ran back to the pile, picked up a piece of brick and threw it straight at him.

Arthur didn’t appear to move, but the brick missed him and bounced across the floor until it hit the far wall. For a second I was sure it had gone straight through him. Chelsea was just standing, eyes wide and mouth open. We looked at each other, astonished. When we looked back, he’d gone, disappeared.

‘Let’s get out of here,’ I shouted and, in panic, we both clambered through the gap into the light of a normal day.

Eight

I swigged Coke from the can. Chelsea sipped at half a glass. We were sitting in the living room. We each had a packet of crisps. I'd hooked up my *PlayStation* to the main TV and I was playing a *Formula1*™ racing game, but I wasn't really concentrating.

'I told you it was spooky,' Chelsea said.

'Spooky nothing. I'm sure I hit the old devil. Direct hit. Couldn't see how he dodged that.'

'But where did he go to?'

'Dunno. But he's always been sneaky and bogged off just when I was gonna do him.'

'But he couldn't have gone. Just like that. So fast. He couldn't have got out of the room. I only looked at you for a second. Did you see him go?'

'Nah. I was looking at you. Then when I looked again he was gone.'

'He just seemed to disappear. On the spot. Gone. He did it when we first met him. Remember? Said his name was Arthur. Then the next moment he was gone. Disappeared into thin air. And we searched the building and he was nowhere to be seen. He couldn't have got out so fast. He couldn't have just gone like that unless...'

'Unless what?'

'I don't know. I mean – unless he wasn't real…'

'Course he was real. Told us he was a Caretaker. Sat there with that pipe as real as you and me.'

'But that's been bugging me. He had the pipe in his mouth, but it wasn't lit and yet we could smell the smoke. And another thing. Why would he say he was a Caretaker when the Hall is obviously derelict and hasn't had a caretaker for years? Unless he was the Caretaker before, when…'

'When what? This is getting boring.'

'When… he was alive!'

'Wha'd'ya mean?'

'Don't you see, Craig? He appears from nowhere. Disappears to nowhere. Says he's the Caretaker. And something else a bit strange which I couldn't place. It's been nagging at me. But then I realised the way he's dressed is a bit old fashioned. Not like Mr Forbes, our caretaker at school. And he said something a bit odd as well. What was it? Caretakers can take care of people as well as places. I think he's not alive. I think he's a ghost, a spirit trapped in that Hall.'

'You're nuts, Chelsea! He didn't seem like any flippin' ghost to me. He's about as scary as my grandma.'

'But perhaps he doesn't want to scare you. Perhaps he just can't leave that place. My mum said ghosts are spirits of dead people which get trapped in this world and don't know they're dead.'

'He had the flippin' cheek to say I was scared. Well I'll show him who's scared if he doesn't get out of our Hall! I'll make him go to another place!'

'No, Craig. I think he's here for a reason and I think we should try to find out what it is.' Chelsea was going on a bit and I was getting fed up.

'He's just squatting, that's all.'

There was silence. Chelsea seemed to be thinking. I just rescued my Ferrari from crashing off the track. Then Chelsea said:

'It's nearly eight o'clock. I'd better be going. Mum will start getting worried. See you tomorrow at school.'

I saw Chelsea out of the door. It would be hours before mum got back. Now that I was alone, I started thinking about what Chelsea had said. Why would the old man be living in that Hall? There was no water, no heating, nothing. It was just a wreck of a place. And when I started thinking about it I realised he wasn't dressed like a tramp. In fact now that I was thinking about it I remembered something that had been bugging me. Why were his boots so highly polished? They couldn't be like that with all that dust and rubble around.

My Ferrari crashed off the track with a high pitched squealing of tyres and a crash like thunder. It brought me back to my senses. I wasn't concentrating. I could only think about Arthur and what Chelsea had said. Turning off the *PlayStation*, I disconnected it from the TV. It was true. One moment he was there, next he was gone. Could he be a ghost? I was feeling nervous now. As my mum had said to me many times, "There you go again, frightening yourself. Frightened of your own shadow you are!" I used to hate her saying that because I never wanted anyone saying that I was frightened of anything. The whole house was quiet. I held my breath and listened for any sounds. I wished my mum was back. Now I could hear a tap-tapping sound and then a motor bike roared down the street. Had I shut the front door properly? I knew I had. I knew it. But, I just had to go and check. I left the front room, and glanced nervously down the hall. I checked the door. It was firmly shut. Going back to the front room I felt I had to look up the stairs. Something white flashed across the landing. Or did it? Was it just the movement of my head as I turned back into the room? I stepped back into the room quickly and shut the door. I stood still and listened. There was the tapping noise again. I was getting frightened. Then annoyed and angry at Chelsea for going on about ghosts and the old man. There were no such things. What did my mum say to Mary when she was going on about that programme, *Most Haunted*. She said, "It's not the Dead you need to be frightened of Mary. It's the Living!"

I had to find out what the tapping was. Slowly I moved out of the room into the hall. I was looking all around, half expecting Arthur to be standing just behind me. I listened hard. The tapping seemed to be coming from the kitchen. Once I was in the kitchen it was louder. Moving across to the sink I could then see that it was only the dripping of the tap. I went over and turned the tap. It went the wrong way and I suddenly jumped back as the water gushed out and splashed hard into the sink. Quickly I turned it hard and waited to make sure it wasn't dripping. I was relieved. It was like my mum says to Mary, *"There's an explanation for everything"*.

Returning to the front room, I checked everywhere as I went, looking into the cupboard under the stairs, looking upstairs to make sure there wasn't anyone there and finally going into the front room and closing the door. I flopped onto the settee. It was still too quiet and it couldn't stop me listening for any little noise. It couldn't stop me thinking about the old man appearing and disappearing. So I put the TV on loud. But it was a boring soap. I flicked through the channels. Cookery programme. Boring! Buying houses programme. Boring! Chat Show. Boring! Game Show. Boring, boring, boring! I flicked on further. Spanish football. No! Golf. No! Tennis. No! *WWE – Late Night Raw*. Yes! I sat and watched the wrestling. As the giant *Umaga* did a *Samoan Drop* on *Bobby Lashley* I didn't think much about Arthur and the Gospel Hall.

The wrestling went on until eleven o'clock. It was now ten. I knew it'd be better if I was in bed before my mum came back. She could get back at any time. When she was late coming in, she was sometimes in a bad mood. If I wasn't in bed she'd tell me off or ground me for a day or two. So now I thought I'd better go to my room and watch a DVD on my telly there. I loved *Antz.* It made me laugh. I've watched it twenty times. I thought it would be the best thing to make me forget the old Caretaker and my mum.

Propped up on my pillow I watched the DVD. After a while, I don't know how long, my eyes got tired, they began to close and I was falling asleep. It was then that I saw him. Sitting at the bottom of my bed. Arthur! He was smiling and looking at me. I wasn't frightened.

'Don't worry, Craig. You needn't be frightened of anything. I'm here to help you.'

I tried to speak but no words came out of my mouth. I could only lie there and listen.

'I am an angel. A Guardian Angel. Your Guardian Angel. I am only here to help you.'

'You can't be.' The words seemed to jump out of my mouth. 'Angels are shiny and bright and they have wings.'

'Some do. They are the *First Angels*. The Highest Order of Angels. They were made in Heaven and stay there. They only visit here at special times. But there are other angels. Some angels who have been here many times before, come and go from Heaven to Earth. But I am a Guardian Angel. When we leave our bodies for the very first time, we cannot go to Heaven until we have helped someone who lives on Earth. Until their life improves. I am a Guardian Angel and I am assigned to you, to help you.'

'But I don't need nobody's help.'

'You do, Craig! You're angry and frightened so you hurt other people. I am here to show you that there is another way.'

Once again I wanted to shout at him but nothing came from my mouth. He stood up. He began to fade. I could see the yellow flowers on the wallpaper through his body. Then he turned and simply walked through the wall.

The next thing I knew was that there was the sound of heavy footsteps coming up the stairs. My eyes opened. I was awake and I was frightened. Who or what was coming up the stairs, closer and closer? Then I heard an angry voice shouting,

'Craig! Turn that telly down! D'you know what time it is? You should be asleep!'

It was mum and she'd had too much to drink. I knew what I had to do. I closed my eyes and pretended to be asleep. As the door flew open I started to make big breathing sounds.

'You little…'

She stopped and looked at me. She must have thought I was really asleep and didn't want to wake me up. Not that she was bothered about disturbing me, more that she wanted me asleep while she went to bed herself. So she quickly turned off the DVD and telly and crept out of the room.

I meant to sit up and look around and see if Arthur was really there, but I knew it was only a dream because mum had woken me up and the telly had still been on and I know I hadn't seen any of *Antz.* I think it was a dream. It must have been. At the time it had seemed real, but it couldn't have been. Anyway, my eyes were tired and I didn't feel like sitting up. So I closed them again and soon I was dreaming. Tom and Adrian and me were in the Hall and Joe had fallen through the balcony. Then, from the pile of rubble, he rose and flew towards us. He was sparkling and had white, feathery wings. He hovered in the air above us saying, " It was you who did it to me, Craig! You! And now I am your Guardian Angel!"

"No you're not! There's no such thing!" I shouted. We all tried to run away. Tom and Adrian lifted the plank and climbed out. But as hard as I tried, I could not move. My legs were moving but I was going nowhere. It was like being stuck in mud. And then coming towards me was Chelsea but she had horns on her head and red eyes and sharp fangs.

"It's too late, Craig! You didn't believe in the Guardian Angel. You didn't want him. So now you're mine. You have to come with me–ee–ee– "

I was frightened and I shouted, "I can't go with you. I can't…" Suddenly, I was awake. Light came in through the curtains. It was morning.

I knew my mum would not be up until later. She never got up before ten when she'd been out drinking with Mary. Usually I had to get myself ready, get my own breakfast and take some money for crisps at break time. School said we had to do healthy eating and take some fruit or a piece of vegetable for snacks. But I never did. I liked crisps and sweets and chocolates best so I always took them. Besides my mum never had much fruit in the house.

So I quickly got undressed in the bathroom, had a quick shower and dried myself. Then I got dressed.

I had some blackcurrant cordial, a *Lion Bar* and a packet of salt and vinegar crisps for my breakfast. Grabbing some coins from my mum's purse which was on the kitchen table, I set off for school.

Nine

In assembly Mr Dawson was telling us about when Jesus went up to Heaven to be with God. He told us how this was after the story of Jesus being killed and then coming alive again. I was beginning to get fed up and I yawned. Miss Denton looked at me, frowning. I put my chin in my hands and closed my eyes.

'Remember in the story I told you at Easter, before we broke up, that Mary and Mary Magdalene went to the tomb which was empty and an angel appeared to them…'

Suddenly I opened my eyes again. Mr Dawson had mentioned an angel. I was listening hard now but he went back to the story of Jesus going up to Heaven. Then it was time to say prayers.

When I got back to class I couldn't settle. I was still thinking about the dream I'd had. It was a dream. I'm sure. I was still a bit bothered and I couldn't think about anything else. In maths I was in a small group with a Learning Assistant. Chelsea was working on hard stuff with the top group. Our group was working out shopping bills like: tin of beans – 39p, tea bags – £1.32, sliced loaf – 85p – how much altogether? All that I wanted to do was talk to Chelsea. Tell her about my dream.

At first I kept calling Chelsea's name. The Learning Assistant said in a quiet voice, 'Come on, Craig! Stop that! We're here to do some maths. Write the list down like I've shown you in the example. Put each amount exactly underneath each other.'

'But, Miss, I don't like these sums!'

'Well, they're to help you to be able to work out how much your shopping will cost when you go to the supermarket.'

'But the girl on the till always does that with that scanner thing. My mum just gives her the money,' I argued.

'But your mum will know what it comes to so that she has enough money, and so that she doesn't spend too much.'

'She just uses a card most of the time so I don't think she cares.' I laughed my silly laugh so that all the others in the group would laugh as well.

'That's enough, Craig! Get on with it!'

'He can't, Miss,' said Tony Roberts, 'because he can't stop thinking about his girlfriend, Chelsea.'

'That is enough, Tony Roberts!'

'Yes. That's enough you monkey-faced, little rat sod.' Tony had made me angry. 'Shut your big, fat gob!' I picked up my ruler and whacked him across the fingers. Tony yelled out all high and squeaky like a pig in pain. Miss heard the noise, left the top group and walked straight over.

'What is going on Miss Jones?'

'Well, Craig won't get on with his sums and Tony has to make silly comments and Craig hit him with the ruler.'

'Craig! Craig! It's always me that gets done! What about him! That flippin' little Tony started it. He…'

'That will do, Craig!' said Miss in her slow, serious voice. 'You cannot behave like this in a classroom! Please leave the room! You will have to work outside! And you, Tony Roberts, will see me at playtime to explain your silly behaviour!'

'Me! Me! Always me!' I screamed. 'Don't want to stay in this stinking old classroom anyway!' Once I'd started, I couldn't stop. I couldn't calm down straight away. Nobody blamed me for doing nothing! Nobody! I flung my pencil at Jacob Jackson because I didn't like his grinning face. I threw my book onto the floor. I rushed across the room, flung open the door and then slammed it shut as hard as I could. Then I flung myself to the floor and sat cross-legged in the corridor with my chin in my hands. I was muttering to myself, 'Always get the blame in this flamin' school! Hate it! Hate it! I'm not coming anymore! Sooner be at home! It's soft! Stupid! Bloomin' teachers! Bloomin', bloomin' Jacob Jackson! I'll fix him one day; stupid, goofy-faced *Gollum*!' That made me laugh out loud to myself.

Later the door opened and Laura Banks came out with her stupid looking ponytail and her silly freckles.

'Where'd you think you're going, spotty face?' I stuck my legs out to stop her.

'Going to get Mr Dawson! Because you've caused trouble again!' She jumped round my legs and trotted off.

'Listen to Miss Perfect! Miss Spotty Perfect! Go and get flippin' Mr Dawson! See if I care a tutti-fruitti! He can't do nothing to me! Silly old Dawson with his big, posh voice!' Then I went to the keyhole, crouched down and began shouting through it. 'Get Mr Dawson! Get Mr Dogson! See if I care! Old Dogson! Dogson! Doggy, doggy, Dogson!' I began rapping on the door in rhythm, chanting, 'Come on you Dogson! Come on, you, Dogson!' It reminded me of watching football on telly so I jumped up at the window and started singing, *"I'm Dogson 'til I die! I'm Dogson 'til I die! I know I am, I know I am, I'm Dogson 'til I die!"*

There was only Adrian inside the classroom who was taking any notice. He was half standing at his desk, waving his arms above his head and swaying from side to side. But Miss told him off and he sat down again. Fed up, I slid down the wall again. I really didn't know why I'd got so angry. I only wanted to talk to Chelsea about Arthur and angels. I didn't want to do any work. It was much more important than stupid shopping bills; just to make you do maths. But I really wanted to still be in class because I needed to talk to Chelsea. It wasn't my fault. If that stupid Tony'd kept his mouth shut I wouldn't have got angry, and got sent out.

I sat still for a moment. Then I thought about what my mum would say to me when she found out I'd been in trouble again. I really didn't want to go home. If I got sent home she'd be really mad. So I decided to sit still and calm myself down. Normally, I would have just run out of school and gone home. But I didn't want to go home because I knew I'd be in big trouble. Most of the time mum lets me do what I want. And I know if I keep going on and on and bothering her, she'll give in to me in the end. But when it spoils her peace and quiet or gives her work to do, she gets really mad and I cop it bad.

I was ripping a piece of paper I'd found on the floor into tiny pieces, when I saw Mr Dawson's shiny shoes just in front of me. I just looked down at the floor and pretended that he wasn't there.

'What are you doing out here, Craig? Why aren't you in class doing your work?'

'Work! Work! Stupid work! That's all there ever is!'

'Why, Craig?'

'Got sent out for nothing!'

'No, Craig! Pupils don't get sent out of a classroom for no reason. I'll ask you again. What have you been doing to get sent out here?'

'It wasn't my fault! It was that Tony Roberts!'

'Tell me what happened, Craig.'

'Tony shouted out that Chelsea is my girlfriend. And she isn't! '

'Why were you not working?'

'Didn't get chance! That Tony bugged me!'

'So what did you do, Craig?'

'Hit him on the knuckles with a ruler. That'll teach the little brat!' I smiled one of my cheeky smiles.

'No! It isn't funny! And we do not use that kind of language in our school. I think it might be better if you came and worked in my room if you cannot work in your own classroom. Don't you?'

'No! Don't want! I want to go back in class.'

'So, what do you need to do, if you go back into the classroom?'

'Dunno!'

'Craig, if you carry on like this, you will have to come with me and I will have to phone your mother.'

''S'not fair! I've not done anything! I don't want to go home. You won't tell my mum. I don't want to go!'

'Then if you stay here, you must behave and do your work. I will phone your mum if you don't go back in and behave like a pupil of this school.'

'All right! All flippin' right!' I threw the bits of ripped paper into the air.

'That is not the right attitude. Now when you go into class what do you need to do?'

'Work!' I said in a snappy voice.

'Your work. Yes. But what do you need to do first for the trouble you have caused?'

'Not do it again!' I knew Mr Dawson wanted me to say sorry to Miss Denton. But I didn't like saying sorry to anybody. Because everybody blamed me for everything, so why should I say sorry.

'Before that, Craig?'

I clenched my fists tight. Why didn't he make Tony Roberts say sorry to me? I felt like just running away from him. But then I remembered my mum.

'Say sorry to Miss,' I said in a quiet voice like when I don't like something and I'm grumbling.

'What was that, Craig?'

'Sorry!' I said in a sudden loud voice. 'Sorry, sorry, sorry!'

'That'll do! Stop it! You go in and say it properly. As if you mean it. Then do not cause any more trouble. Nothing!' Mr Dawson took me back into the classroom. 'Craig has something to say to you, then he is going to behave for the rest of the day and do his work. He can come to me at playtime to show me his work. I am hoping to see some good work, Craig. If he cannot behave properly please send for me again. And we know what happens then, don't we Craig?'

'Sorry, Miss Denton.'

'Well I hope you are, Craig. Thank you Mr Dawson. I've finished with my group. They are getting on by themselves so you can join them, Craig, and I'll help you catch up with what you've missed. Come along.'

Miss sat with me and showed me how to do the shopping sums. I did one and got it right. It was easy. I was happier now because I was sitting near Chelsea. I did the next sum by myself. That was right too.

'Now Craig, see if you can do the next three. You seem to have got the hang of it. You're doing well. I have to go and check on the other groups and then I'll be back to see how you've done.'

As soon as she had gone, I said to Chelsea in a quiet voice, 'I've got something to tell you about the old bloke in the Hall…'

'You mean Arthur,' whispered Chelsea.

'Yeh. Him.'

'Better tell me at break then nobody else can hear. And if you don't get those sums done, Miss Denton and Mr Dawson might not let you go out.' Chelsea put her head down and got on with her worksheet.

I stopped talking and got on with my sums. Miss came back just as I was finishing my last sum. She checked them all and I'd got them all right. Miss Denton gave me one team point and a sticker which had a picture of a lion on it and around the edges the words *"Good Work"*.

'Well done, Craig! See what you can do when you try. Now the bell is going to go in two minutes for playtime. So if you take your work down to Mr Dawson now and show him, I'm sure he'll be very pleased and let you go out to play.'

I felt good. I was smiling. So I thought I'd ask Miss something.

'Miss, in assembly, Mr Dawson told us about them angels that the two women saw. But what's a Garden Angel?'

'A Garden Angel? Garden Angel? I don't think… Wait … Do you mean a Guardian Angel?'

'Yeh, Miss. A Guardian Angel.'

'Well, a Guardian Angel is supposed to look after people here on Earth. Everyone's supposed to have one but most people never see them. People think they look after you and, if you ask them, they will help you.'

'Oh! Thank you, Miss.'

Ten

Mr Dawson was pleased with my work. He gave me another team point and one of his special Head Teacher stickers. It was blue with a golden crown in the middle. He said that I could go straight out to playtime.

As soon as Chelsea came into the playground, I headed straight for her. Luckily, Adrian and Tom were more interested in a game of football against another class. I didn't like football that much. Every time I played, someone fouled me and a fight started and I usually got sent in. So Chelsea and me went and sat on a bench in one corner of the playground.

'What's all this about an angel that you were asking Miss Denton? And, do you want to tell me about Arthur? You've not told anybody what I said…?'

'No! Course not! Who'd believe me anyway? Just listen, last night, I thought I saw him…'

'In your house? After I'd gone? You mean he came to your house?'

'No! Yes! I dunno! I mean that I had a dream. When you'd gone and I'd watched a bit of wrestling, I thought I'd better be in bed before my mum got back. Anyway, I had my telly on in bed with a DVD, you know *Antz*, I like that one. I've watched it loads of times. I don't remember much after that because I must have fallen asleep. And I had this dream and he was in it. Him, the old man, Arthur! He was sitting at the bottom of my bed. Just sitting there, smiling. Then he said,

“Don’t be frightened. I’m here to help you. I am a Guardian Angel.” And then, in my dream, he walked away, through the wall. That’s when my mum came in and heard the telly on dead loud. That’s when I woke up. I think. I’m sure. But it was like, dead real, as if he’d actually been there.’

Chelsea’s face went very pale. She looked like she was ill. I thought she was going to cry.

‘What’s the matter? Don’t you believe me?’

‘I just feel a bit weird, that’s all. This is all a bit spooky. My mum’s interested in all this psychic stuff. She’s done séances. Ever since dad died, I think, but I don’t know because I was too young. But things are happening which are stranger than all that.’

‘What? Just because I had a dream about the old squatter?’

‘Not just that, Craig. You see, last night, I had a dream too. It was weird and scary.’

‘Don’t tell me you had a dream about him as well.’

‘No! Well, I’m not sure. In my dream I was lying in a bed, dozing off to sleep and then my body lifted up and I was floating around the room. Suddenly it was like a magnet was pulling me and I was rushing towards the ceiling. Then the ceiling wasn’t there and I was in a whirling tunnel. Like being inside a tornado, I suppose. I was struggling to escape but it was too strong. I screamed but no sound came. In the next moment it slowed down and I was floating towards a bright, silvery light and I didn’t want to escape any more. I felt relaxed and happy. But then somebody came to me. I couldn’t tell who because the person was wobbly and like a shadow. He or she took hold of my hand and pulled me along. Then a door opened and I was back in my bed in my room. I woke up and it was morning.’

‘See! You and your ghosts! You’ve got us both dreaming about ghosts and Guardian Angels.’

‘I’ve never mentioned anything about angels. Let alone Guardian Angels! Who’s been telling you about that?’

‘Nobody! It was in the flippin’ dream. I told you. He said he was a Guardian Angel. My Guardian Angel. And he can’t leave here until he’s helped somebody here on earth. And that somebody’s flippin’ me!’

‘Then that’s what it means! That’s why he came to us in the Gospel Hall. He’s here to help you.’

‘But it was only a dream. It wasn’t real.’

‘I don’t know about that, Craig.’ Then the whistle went for the end of playtime and we all went in, class by class.

The rest of the day at school went without any problems. Well, except that after playtime in the afternoon, Carly Burton told on me for pinching her skipping rope and tying her friend, soppy Kirsty, to a railing. The teacher on duty told Miss Denton at the end of playtime. Why can’t teachers keep their noses out of other people’s business? Anyway, we had a lesson in the computer suite and Miss Denton wanted to get it started. She’s always in a rush when she’s got to do computers with us. She asked me about it but said playtime had ended and the time for fussing over it was gone and that we were in class for more important work. She was always nervous when it was computers because she didn’t like it if they went wrong. If it had been any other lesson, she would have gone on about it and sent for other children until she found out what had happened. But luckily it was computers so by the end of the day, she’d forgotten about it.

I left school at the end of the day and went straight to the Gospel Hall. But no one was there and I was by myself. There was not much to do except throw a few stones at a rusty old bucket which was sticking up from the long grass. I didn’t want to go inside. I wasn’t scared, but I didn’t want to go inside by myself. Then I remembered my sticker. I wanted to go straight home then because I wanted to show my mum. I ran home, through the door and it was only when I walked into the living room and asked for a packet of crisps, that I knew something was wrong.

Standing with her arms folded, in a way that I knew that I was going to be told off, Mum held a piece of paper in her hand.

'Do you know what this is?' she said. She screwed up her mouth in a shape like when you whistle, but instead she said in a lower voice, 'This is a letter from school, Craig. It's from Mr Dawson about a meeting in two weeks' time…'

I turned away and looked through the window as if she wasn't there, as if I hadn't heard her. I do that sometimes when I am being told off. I didn't say anything.

'Craig! Craig! I'm speaking to you. You'd better listen.' Then just like Mr Dawson, she said, 'Look at me, Craig. I – said – look – at – me – now!' I looked and shrugged my shoulders. 'This is a meeting about your behaviour. I haven't had any phone calls recently from Mr Dawson, and now there's going to be a big meeting with Mr Dawson, Social Services and lots of other people. Are you still causing trouble?'

'I got a sticker today for doing good work from Mr Dawson. Tony Roberts tried to wind me up, but…'

'Never mind the sticker, have you been in trouble with Mr Dawson?'

'Only because that Tony Roberts kept saying Chelsea was my girlfriend. I said sorry to Miss Denton and did all my sums. I got them all right, and Mr Dawson gave me a sticker.'

'What did you do to Tony Roberts? C'mon, Craig, I need to know.'

'I only tapped him on the knuckles with a ruler. He wasn't even hurt.'

'Here we go again! Losing your temper and hurting others. No wonder they've called a meeting. We've both got to go. Craig, will you never learn?'

'I'm not going to no silly meeting.'

'You will be going. It's to help you and me. I can't cope any longer with all of this nonsense. Something's got to be done before you get expelled!'

'I'm not going! It's not fair! I got a sticker today.'

'That's a start, Craig, But we've seen all of this before. One day you're good and the next you're back in trouble.'

'Can I go out playing after tea?'

'There you go again, changing the subject. The answer is NO! You can stay in and watch TV with me. I won't be going out and leaving you, anymore. Not when you're getting out of control and getting into trouble at school.'

'No, I'm not! I'm going out!'

'You're grounded tonight.'

'I want to go out, I want to go out!'

'Don't you start all that nonsense with me. You might think that you can behave like that at school, but it doesn't work with me. You will go up to you room and you can have your tea up there. And you won't be going out to play!'

'I want to go out, I want to go out!' I kept shouting as I stomped up the stairs. I slammed my bedroom door and letting out a loud cry, I dived onto my bed. 'I want to go out!' I shouted.

There was no answer…

I threw my pillow onto the floor. I began chanting, ***"I want to go out"***, silence… I decided that it wasn't fair and quietly, like a burglar, I started to creep down the stairs.

I could hear the TV in the living room, and thought that it would be easy for me to escape. Mum wouldn't even notice. I got to the fourth step and it creaked. Scared; I stood still. She hadn't heard me. I carried on down the stairs, trying not to make a sound and then, when I reached the last step, I ran really fast to the front door, turned the handle and pulled. It was locked! Thinking about the back door, I leaped past the living room door and ran as fast as I could to the kitchen. I grabbed for the handle, but... Locked! From the living room, Mum shouted, 'It's no use, Craig, the doors are locked. Go back to your room and I'll bring you your tea.'

'IT'S NOT FAIR!' I shouted, as I ran back up to my room.

I flung myself onto the bed and lay there with a comic, tearing pages out of it and scattering them all around the room.

'Don't want no tea! Won't eat it! Won't eat it!'

A few minutes later, mum brought up my tea. She put it on the desk.

'Eat your tea. You can come down and watch telly when you've finished.'

It was beans, beef burger and oven chips, with a blob of tomato sauce.

'Don't want it! Won't eat it!' I called after her, as she turned and closed the door. Mum didn't say anything. She just went downstairs. She didn't argue or shout back. That annoyed me. I don't like it when I can't argue back.

Now I was in a really bad mood. I roared in my loudest voice. I screamed for about thirty seconds. But mum just ignored me. I was mad. I bit my own knuckles and clenched my fist. I jumped up, ripped my wrestling poster from the wall, scattered books and knocked my model cars and aeroplanes off the desk. Then I pushed the plate of food across the desk. It crashed against the side of my wardrobe. Chips and burger fell onto the carpet. Beans were spread everywhere.

'Don't want no tea!' I shouted.

I heard mum coming up the stairs, shouting '*Blood and Sand!* What on earth is going on?'

The door flew open. She stood and looked. She didn't move. I sat on my bed end, staring at her with my meanest look.

'I want to go out! I want to go out!'

Mum couldn't speak at first. She just looked at the mess. Then she began to sniffle. Then there was a sobbing noise. She was crying. Proper crying. With tears running down her face. I'd only seen her cry like this once before, when the police took my dad away in their car. In between the crying she was saying, 'This – is – too – much. Look – look – at – this – mess! I – can't – can't – take – anymore. I – don't – don't want you – anymore! I – want – you – in a special – home. I – want – them to take – take you – AWAY!'

'No, mum, no!'

Now I began to cry. I didn't want to be taken anywhere else. In that instant I knew what I'd done. 'Don't mum, don't – I'll – I'll…'

It was then that I heard him. Arthur. I looked round. There was nobody there. But there was this voice in my head.

'Craig, you must stop this. You must say you're sorry. You must clear up this mess. You must help your mum. You must stop being angry.' Then it was gone.

I looked at mum who was still sobbing and I knew that she hadn't heard the voice. I knew that it was only me who had heard him. Or, was it just in my own thoughts.

'Stop it, mum! Please! I'm sorry! I'm sorry! I don't want to be taken away. I want to stay here, with you. I'll be good! I will! I'll clear all this up!'

She let me lead her, with her hands over her face, still crying, and sit her on the bed.

'I'll clear it up now. I will. I won't never do it again. Honest!'

Still crying, she stood up and said, 'I don't know what to do with you, Craig. I don't know where you'll end up.'

She was sniffing as she crossed to the door. And all that she said as she left the room, was, 'You'd better clear it up! You better had!'

I went downstairs and got a dust pan and brush and cloths and cleaning stuff. It took me an hour to straighten up and clean up the room.

That night I went to bed early and I don't know if mum had looked in to see what my room was like. I had lost my temper, and for once I knew I shouldn't have. I was sorry. I'd done what Arthur had said. I had done what my "Guardian Angel" had said. And I felt better afterwards.

Eleven

Dancing up and down, the little flames on the ten candles dripped bits of wax onto the pink icing of the cake. Written in white icing on top of the pink, it said, *"Happy Birthday Chelsea"*. On a little plastic stand there was a picture of *Hannah Montana*, Chelsea's favourite pop singer. I had been invited to Chelsea's tenth birthday party, along with some of her friends, four girls from our class and two other boys, Steven Harris and Ben Blackley and two of her cousins.

I was just going to blow out the candles before Chelsea could. I thought it would be a good joke and besides I'd not had candles and a cake on my birthday – not even a party. But I looked at Chelsea bending forward to blow and then at her mother who had her hands together in front of her face, smiling away. Then I looked at everyone all waiting, ready to see her blow out the candles. And I knew I couldn't do it; I knew I shouldn't do it. So I stopped myself and watched Chelsea put out all the candles in one big blow. Everyone clapped and cheered. I joined in. Her cousin, Louise, shouted, 'Make a wish, Chelsea. Now you've got to make a wish but don't tell anyone. Just to yourself.'

Then her mother began to sing, *"Happy Birthday to you"* and we all joined in.

It was Friday, after school, and we were all around the big table in Chelsea's dining room. When we had finished singing,

Chelsea's mother said, 'Now does anybody want anything to eat?' There were shouts of 'Me! Me!' and 'Yes, please!'

Her mother turned to go into the kitchen but then she paused and said, more to herself than to us, 'Oh! What's that smell? It's like – like smoke – like someone smoking a pipe.' She looked round as if to find someone in the room smoking a pipe, then, with a puzzled look and a shake of her head, went into the kitchen. I heard what she said. I could smell the pipe smoke. I looked over to Chelsea, but she was laughing and joking with her cousin so she hadn't heard. Looking round I expected to see Arthur, but there was no one there. Everything was normal.

Then Chelsea's mum brought in trays and plates of sandwiches, cakes, sausage rolls. She also brought crisps, sausages on sticks, jellies and drinks. When she had put down a bowl of trifle with glass dishes and spoons, she stood back and said, 'Come on everyone. Don't be shy. Tuck in!'

Then, folding her arms, she stood back to watch. Normally, I would have made sure what I wanted and pushed in to grab it. Somehow, though, I felt Chelsea's mum was watching me. Had people been telling her that I was a naughty boy who got into trouble? So, I waited. I let Steven Harris take a sausage roll before me. I was putting a sandwich and some crisps on my plate and I felt her mother was still staring at me. I got annoyed when people looked at me like that and I usually said something like, "What do you think you're looking at, Goofy Face?" So I looked up at her. She was staring in my direction but not at me. She was looking hard at somebody or something behind my left shoulder. Slowly and carefully, I looked behind but there was only a picture on the wall. Then she frowned slightly, shook her head and looked back at Chelsea.

'Now all push in together. I want to take a few photos.'

Reaching back to the top of the sideboard, she picked up her digital camera.

'You children at this side, turn round to face me. Louise push in a bit closer to Chelsea. Boys at either end, move in just a touch closer. That's it! Lovely! Now let's have some big smiles.' We stood in a group like that whilst Chelsea's mum took several photos.

Whilst we carried on eating and talking and laughing, she flicked through the photos she'd just taken on the little camera screen. Stuffing a sausage roll into my mouth, I was still watching Chelsea's mum. I didn't want her to think bad things about me, so I kept watching and making sure I was doing nothing wrong. I wanted her to say to Chelsea afterwards, "Isn't that Craig a nice boy?" I never expected my mum to say good things about me, and most of the time I didn't care if teachers or other people said bad things about me. But I liked Chelsea's mum. She was tall and slim and she had short, black hair and dark brown eyes. Chelsea had the same black hair but she had hers in a ponytail. She also had dark brown eyes but she had freckles across her nose and cheeks. Her mum was kind and quiet and didn't shout not even when Ben Blackley spilled his orange juice. She just said, 'Never mind, love. Don't worry about it. It's only a paper tablecloth and I'll soon have it mopped up. Here, give me your glass and I'll get you some more orange.'

I wanted her to like me, so I wanted to show her that I could be a bit like Chelsea. As I kept looking up at her between spoonfuls of jelly, I noticed she kept looking at the same picture on the screen. She didn't click over to the next one. She seemed puzzled and once again she shook her head. Then, after a while, she clicked on through all the other photos.

We ate a lot of food and Chelsea's mum put music on. We played a game of musical statues and I won. I had to dip my hand into a big box covered in shiny gold paper. I pulled out a bag of sweets. Just to show how good I was, I said to Chelsea's mum, 'Thank you. Would you like one?'

'That's very kind, Craig. Thank you. But they're for you. You won them.'

I was in a really good mood, so I went round and offered everyone a sweet. Then we went out into the garden for more games. Chelsea's garden was much bigger than ours. The grass was cut neatly and there were different coloured flowers and bushes and trees. There was a bird bath and a metal bird feeder with nuts and seeds. My small back garden was overgrown. The grass was long and scruffy. The fence was falling down in one part. There was an old sink and pram wheels dumped at the bottom end. There were even bottles and cans thrown into the grass and my mum never moved them. There were weeds everywhere.

Chelsea's mum brought out a large piece of material which had different coloured sections. At first I thought it was an umbrella, but it was a parachute, for parachute games. We played lots of games, going under the parachute, tossing a ball on top of it and running round it. It was great fun. I really enjoyed it.

Then, one by one, parents came to pick up their children and the party began to come to an end. Soon there was only Chelsea and me left.

'Can Craig help us to tidy up Mum?'

'Hasn't he got to get home? His mum might be wondering where he is.'

'I said it only ended at seven thirty, so she won't be expecting me yet. I've got my mobile so I said I'd ring her when it was time to come home.'

'OK then. For a short while. Come on, let's get the dishes into the dishwasher.'

Chelsea and me helped to carry plates to the kitchen whilst her mother loaded the dishwasher. We took rubbish out to the bin and we tidied up. Her mum said we were good helpers and gave us an ice lolly saying, 'Go on, take them into the garden for a short while. Why don't you show Craig your vegetable patch?'

In Chelsea's vegetable patch, in the very bottom corner of the garden next to the shed, were bean plants climbing up cones and twigs. Growing in the soil were different rows of plants, all very small. Chelsea told me there were lettuce, carrots and onions.

Then I sensed something. Like someone was watching me. So I stood up, and looked back at the house. Once again Chelsea's mum was staring at me through the kitchen window, well, not straight at me, but at something to the side of me. I turned to look but there was nothing there. I turned to look back at the window. Her mum saw me and looked down into the sink, then turned away. Melting lolly ran down onto my hand, so I quickly licked it off and put the lolly into my mouth, sucking hard.

'Chelsea,' I said between sucks. 'Did you hear what your mum said just before we started eating?'

'What? About the birthday cake?'

'No. When she said she could smell smoke – pipe smoke. I got a faint whiff of it. Didn't you?'

'No. But do you mean, like Arthur's pipe?'

'Dunno. But she could smell it. And I smelled something. Then she was looking at me, no, not at me, but staring as if there was someone behind me or next to me.'

'Did she say anything? Was there someone…?'

'No. I looked and there was nothing, and no, she never said a word. She just went into the kitchen for the food.'

'Do you think she saw something? Arthur? Have you had any more dreams?'

'No. But…' I was about to tell her about the voice then I stopped. I thought it would only set her off again.

'Something *has* happened, hasn't it? Please tell me Craig. After all it is our secret and I think I should know.'

'Well – well… It was just that my mum was shouting at me to tidy my room and I was refusing and then I heard – well it was a voice – not in the room – in my head and it told me to clear up the mess and help my mum.'

'A voice? Arthur's voice?'

'Yes. Arthur's voice.'

'And did you see him?'

'No. It was just a voice.'

'Well, I wonder… My mum is into all that psychic stuff; I told you that. She sometimes senses things. So, if he was here, at the party, she'd probably have got vibes.'

'And she was looking at one of the photos she took of us. She seemed to be looking at one for quite a bit and she looked a bit worried or something.'

'Come on. I'll get the camera and we'll have a look.'

Whilst her mother was still tidying in the kitchen, we crept into the dining room and Chelsea took the camera from the sideboard. Sitting on the lawn, Chelsea flicked through the photographs and we both studied the pictures on the small screen. Click! The next photo came on. We both stared at each other, then back at the screen, then at each other, then back at the screen. In the photo we were all grouped together, smiling and laughing, but behind me and all round my head and shoulders there were little balls of coloured light.

Twelve

On Monday Chelsea and me had arranged to go to the Gospel Hall after school to see if we could find out any more about Arthur. Chelsea was convinced he was some kind of ghost, but even though I'd had a dream and heard his voice in my head, I couldn't believe it. I was beginning to wish I hadn't told her about my dream or the voice.

During morning playtime, Chelsea had taken me to the quiet bench in the corner of the playground.

'Guess what? Over the weekend Mum's been talking about you.'

'What's she been saying? Has she found out that I keep getting into trouble at school? Who told her? It wasn't you, was it?'

'Don't be daft! No, she wasn't saying anything about things like that. My mum always says to me, "Never judge a book by its cover".'

'What! Does she know I can't read very well?'

'No, no, Craig! She means she just doesn't say bad things about anybody without knowing what they're like. No! She was going on about psychic things. Ever since my dad died when I was little, she's been interested in the Hereafter.'

'Hear what? What's that?'

'The Hereafter. Where we go when we die. She's been interested in spirits and ghosts and things like that. Told me that once my dad appeared to her, as a ghost, and said he was all right and happy.'

'Oooh! Spooky! But what's that got to do with me.'

'Well, she said she saw the faint shape of a man, standing just behind you when we were at the dining table. She told me what you said. That she could smell pipe smoke. And she said the man was old, about seventy or eighty and was quite chubby and nearly bald but with thin strands of white hair across his head. She also said he was wearing an overall with a jacket and had a pipe in his mouth.'

'That's Arthur! But it couldn't have been…'

'Unless Arthur is a ghost! Mum asked me if your granddad had died recently.'

'Nah! He's still alive. Besides he's tall and thin and has a crew cut, a bit like mine…' I pushed back my blond, spiky hair with my hand. 'My mum always said I was the "looker" in our family. Blond hair, blue eyes and the face of an angel is what she always said. And he has an earring and wears glasses and he's always chewing gum.'

'She was wondering if you had told me about seeing things. She said that Psychic Energy must be attracted to you. That you must attract spirits and things like that.'

'No, I flippin' well don't! Only Arthur, and you've seen him and Adrian, Joe and Tom have. You didn't tell her about Arthur and the Gospel Hall?'

'No, of course I didn't! I just acted as if I didn't know what she was talking about.'

Later, after school, as we picked our way through a bed of them Rosey Willows or whatever they're called, Chelsea said, 'I'm going to ask him, straight out, who he is. Why he's here. Why he wants to help you. If he's alive or if he's a – '

'Ghost ! Yeh! An' he's gonna say, "Yes Chelsea. I am a ghost. I haunt this Gospel Hall. I am the Ghost of The Gospel Hall!"'

'No! I'm going to ask him if he's your Guardian Angel. He said he was a Caretaker. What was it he said? "Caretakers can take care of people as well as places." He said he was here to take care of you. But how could he do that, if he was just squatting here? How could he take care of you; at home, in school, anywhere? How? Unless he was your Guardian Angel!'

I pulled back the plank. We went in, but there was nobody in the main hall. We looked at the pile of rubble where the balcony had collapsed. It was just the same as we had left it. Nobody'd ever been in the place. So nobody knew about the balcony falling in.

'Let's go and look in the other rooms,' said Chelsea.

We left the main hall. We searched the corridor and other rooms. Nobody there. We called Arthur's name. Nobody answered. Then we went back into the main hall. Sitting on the crate, in the middle of the hall, Arthur was calmly smoking his pipe. Now we could smell the pipe smoke. We approached, nervously.

'Arthur, Arthur,' Chelsea said quietly. He didn't move. Just kept sucking on his pipe.

So I shouted, 'Arthur, why are you still here, when I told you to get lost?'

Arthur turned his head and looked straight into my eyes.

'Because I'm the Caretaker, and you're still scared and angry. You still need my help.'

'Who are you?' asked Chelsea.

'Told you. Arthur.'

'What are you?' I said in my nastiest voice.

'The Caretaker.'

'We know,' said Chelsea in a kind, soft voice. 'But where do you live?'

'Here and there.'

'Chelsea means, are you alive,' I said in a snappy voice.

'I'm here, aren't I? Talking to you.'

'Why are you here, Arthur?'

'To work. To help.'

'What work?' Chelsea was becoming more bossy in her voice.

'To take care of things. And people. To take care of Craig and help him. To help him, to help you.'

'I don't need your flippin' help!'

'But you do Craig. I've told you I'm here to help you with your fear and anger, so that you can help others too.'

'Help? Me, help? Like who?'

'Yourself. Chelsea. Anybody. Everybody. And to do so, you must lose your fear.'

'I'm not scared of anything!'

'You are scared. Scared of yourself. Scared of failing, of being wrong. Scared of showing your true feelings. Scared of showing love. But my work here is to help you. To show you that you needn't be scared.'

'What a load of cock and bull rubbish!'

'You're even scared to admit that you're scared. We're all frightened of things. At different times. But anger and temper do not drive away the fear. No. They only make it worse.'

'Are you alive, Arthur?' Chelsea asked the question this time.

'I'm alive to you, aren't I?'

'See, it's useless. Talks in riddles. Won't answer properly. I'm not the one that's scared. It's you!'

'Craig!' said Chelsea, softly. 'Let him answer. Just listen. You are alive to us but – '

'I am still in this world. But I have got to go to another place. I can't go until I've helped Craig.'

'You're his Guardian Angel, aren't you?'

'Yes. I am.'

'I don't want no Guardian flippin' Angel! I don't need you! I don't want you! So, why don't you just bog off!'

'Craig! Stop it!' Chelsea didn't shout often. It was the first time she had ever raised her voice to me. 'Arthur is your Guardian Angel. He's here to help you. Anybody else would be happy. And all you can do…'

Just then Arthur began to fade. In front of our eyes. His body seemed to fade like when you turn a dimmer light switch.

'I am only here to help you.' His voice was fading too but I heard him say, quietly now, 'Whenever you feel you need help just call on me. Just call my name.' Then he had gone. The empty crate stood in the middle of the hall.

I knew now that Arthur was a ghost. I knew that when he appeared in my bedroom, I wasn't dreaming. I knew that the voice I heard wasn't just in my head. But I didn't know what to do and I didn't know how much it would mean to me in the end.

'Perhaps he's gone for good,' I said cockily. 'I hope so. I don't want him bugging me all the time.'

'I don't think he has, Craig. You heard what he said, "I can't go until I have helped Craig." He's your *Guardian Angel.* You're the only one who can help him go to the next world.'

Thirteen

Mr Dawson's room wasn't very big. He was sitting behind his desk with two ladies, one on either side of him. I was sitting on one of the blue fold up chairs we used for concerts in the assembly hall. My mum was next to me. In the corner, in front of the computer screen, was our Social Worker. In the opposite corner next to the two filing cabinets, was another lady.

As usual, I didn't look at the people much because I knew they were all going to talk about me and things I had done. So I just tried to ignore them by looking round the room and out of the window. Behind Mr Dawson was a long notice board covered in blue paper with a yellow border. Blue and yellow were our school colours. Stapled to this were lots of big sheets of paper with typing on them and big titles in bold, black capitals. On top of the filing cabinet was a small potted plant, a framed photograph of a school team and a silver trophy. To the left were the windows, and I could see a class playing rounders at the far side of the field. I pushed up a bit from my chair, straining to see what was going on. My mum gave me a nudge and I sat down again. Then, moving along, I saw a monitor high on the wall and it was showing the seating part of the playground. There wasn't anyone in the playground. On the worktop, behind the Social Worker and next to the computer was a joystick. You could use this to move to any area outside and you could zoom in on people. I really liked it. Mr Dawson had let me have a go a few times when I'd been good or done some good work.

Mr Dawson and the two ladies at the desk were looking at some papers and talking quietly. I was getting a bit fed up just sitting there so I said in my nicest voice:

'Mr Dawson, can I have a go at the camera, please?'

Before he could answer my mum said, 'Craig! This is an important meeting about your future and you ask a stupid thing like that.'

'Your mum's right, Craig,' said Mr Dawson. 'We've got a lot to get through and this isn't the right time. But if you work well when you go back to class, then perhaps you can have a go at the beginning of playtime. Now I think we'd better get started. Everybody's here, so I'll hand over to Mrs Stenson who is going to chair this meeting.'

'Thank you, Mr Dawson. First I think we'd better go round the room and introduce ourselves so that everyone knows who is who. I am Mrs Stenson, the Child Liaison Officer for the Local Authority.'

'Mr Dawson, Head Teacher.'

'Mrs Thompson, school's contact officer for the Behavioural Team.'

'Kelly O'Donoghue, the family's Social Worker.'

'Er – Mrs Hartshorn, Craig's mother.'

'Craig. Mr Dawson, my mum's given me my granddad's old guitar and I can play some notes on it. Can I bring it into school?'

'Craig, stop it! I'll take the guitar off you. It's for home not for bringing into school. Oh, what am I going to do with you?'

'But I want to play a tune for Miss Denton and the whole class.'

Mrs Stenson interrupted, 'I'm sure if you ask Mr Dawson and your teacher and your mum later on, then perhaps something can be arranged. But now we must get underway. Mrs Walton…'

'Er – yes. Mrs Walton from the Child Liaison Office. I'm going to take notes of everything said and produce the minutes, a copy of which will be sent to all present.'

'Thank you. The purpose of this meeting is to review Craig's progress and behaviour and make recommendations to bring about improvement. So, first we must hear about the extent of the problems from all settings then we can assess what needs to be done. If we could start with you Mrs Hartshorn. How do you see the problem? How does Craig behave at home? How do you view his behaviour at school? What do you see as the main areas of concern?'

'Well, first, he's a great worry to me,' said Mum. She paused and there was a tear in each eye.

'Take your time. Don't worry. We're here to try and help you,' said Mrs Stenson.

'Well, he gets into bother at school and – and Mr Dawson has to keep sending him home. He says bad things to teachers and Mr Dawson. And when he's excluded he – he promises me he will be good. And he is. For a day or two and then he starts again.'

I made sure I was watching the rounders outside. I didn't want to hear all this bad stuff about me. It wasn't always my fault. Somebody else usually sets me off. Sometimes it's Miss; she gets on at me all the time.

'He runs out of class. He shouts and screams at people. He won't do any work and he's way behind the others. I'm at my wits' end…' My mum took out a tissue and dabbed at her eyes. '…He calls teachers rude names and calls out in class and has even turned tables and chairs over. And he's always getting into fights. But there's others who wind him up and Craig's got this temper. He doesn't know how to control it and he ends up hurting other children, but they get away with it sometimes because they've started it. I don't really think he can cope in a big class or a big school…'

'So what do you think should be done?'

'I've told him he'll get sent to a Special School for naughty boys. Perhaps that's what should happen! They are smaller and know how to deal with kids like Craig. I can't go on no longer with this…'

'I'm not going to no Special School! None of you can make me!'

'Now, Craig, nobody's sending anybody, anywhere. We're going to try and do some things to help you control your temper so that you can get on better in class and not get into so much trouble,' said Mrs Stenson. 'But you must do your bit. You must try hard not to lose your temper.'

I calmed down a bit and just sat still, staring up at the ceiling with my "I'm not listening" look on my face.

'And, Mrs Hartshorn, what's he like at home?'

Mum was sniffing. She wiped her eyes again with a tissue. 'Mo – most of the time you don't know he's there. And he can be really nice and polite. But if I tell him to be in the house of an evening at a certain time, he'll just ignore me and come in when he wants. If I tell him to get off the computer at bed time, he won't and then he starts shouting. The other night he wrecked his room because I wouldn't let him go out. And sending him home from school all the time when he's naughty, doesn't work because he won't do any work at home and he's getting further and further behind.'

The lady looked at me.

'Are you naughty at home for your mum sometimes?' I looked back at her. I didn't like baby questions. I just smiled.

'No! Only when she gets on at me and won't let me play on my *PlayStation* or wants me to come in dead early. And that's not fair because she goes out and doesn't come in early.'

'Craig!' said my mum in her most serious voice.

'Well I don't like being nagged all the time.'

'None of us like that, Craig. But sometimes it might be for your own good. And do you lose your temper when you get nagged?'

'Yeh! Good and proper! If my mum shouts, then I shout louder!'

'What else do you do when you get angry?'

'It makes me want to bash things and break things and just run out of the way.'

'And what makes you angry at school, Craig?'

'Miss Denton. She always blames me because she doesn't like me. She always gets on at me when that bloomin' big head softy, Jacob Jackson, bugs me.'

'What does this Jacob do to you?'

'He looks at me with his funny, ugly face.' I crossed my eyes in a funny face and laughed.

'Craig, this is serious. Tell the lady properly,' my mum said.

'Well he does. He's always pulling faces at me and he tells on me and he calls me names and he kicks me under the table. Then, because I throw a pencil at him or a rubber, Miss shouts at me and blames me…'

'And what happens then?'

'Well, I just go.'

'Go? Where Craig?'

'Out of the class! Out of the school! Out of her flippin' way!'

'Craig, stop being so rude. Stop it! Now! This is how he treats me sometimes with his rudeness and nastiness.'

'Your mum's right, Craig. You can't just say things like that about people. It can be very serious. But that will do. We must move on. Next we'll hear from your Social Worker, then we'll have school's viewpoint and finally the input of the Local Authority.'

I stopped listening again.

Things seemed to go on and on. Talk, talk, talk! I was bored. Then finally, the stupid meeting finished. And that posh Mrs Stenson said to me, 'I hope you understand all that Craig. What you must do and what might happen if you don't. Do you?'

I just sat there. I didn't want to answer her stupid question.

'Craig!' said my mum, nudging me.

'Yes.' Then louder, 'Yes!'

'Well, I hope so, because you've got to really try now. You've been given a chance to show how well you can behave. I want to hear good news from Mr Dawson.'

It was only afterwards, when all the others had gone that my mum, with Mr Dawson, told me what would happen. The only bit I'd really listened to was when my Social Worker, Kelly, had said that when I went with her every Tuesday to the special activities, I was always pleasant, polite and well behaved. She said that whether it was swimming, or basketball, or a trip to *McDonald's*, I always got on with the other children.

Anyway Mr Dawson told me that my Social Worker was going to continue with the weekly evenings out because they seemed to bring out my good behaviour. He said that, in school, I was going to be on a behaviour thing, where I had to say five things that I was going to do to improve my behaviour and I would get a point for each one and at the end of the week my mum would see this card thing telling her how many good behaviour points I'd got. If I didn't get many then there would be a meeting. If I got a lot I would get a reward. He also said that if I had to be excluded, then I wouldn't be sent home but I'd go to this Unit Class Place at the High School which only took six children at a time and where you had to do work all day and even have your dinner in the same room. He also said, that if I didn't behave there or if I kept getting excluded, I would have to go to a Special Unit and I'd have to do three days there and two in school and I wouldn't be able to see my friends at school for those three days. Mrs Thompson would be coming into school once a week to work with me and a small group to see how we could stop being angry.

All this made me forget about Arthur and whether he was a Guardian Angel or not, until something happened which made me remember him.

Fourteen

It was the very next day after school that Arthur's words came into my mind, "If you need help call on me. Just call my name."

Adrian, Tom and Joe had all gone to cricket practice after school. I'd wanted to go to have a mess about, but Mr Hughes had said I was banned because last time I had caused trouble – so he said! It was because I was batting and I wasn't ready and Sean Turner bowled before I was ready. Everybody shouted, *"Howzat"* when the ball hit the wickets. Mr Hughes said, 'Next batsman in please.' But I said, 'I'm not out! I wasn't ready!'

Mr Hughes said, 'Craig, give the bat to Robert.'

'No! I wasn't out!' I shouted. 'I – was – *not* – out! He bowled when I wasn't ready! Not out! Not out!'

'I am the umpire, Craig. Not you! Now give the bat to Robert.'

'It's not fair! It's not fair!' I shouted and then I started chanting, 'Cheat! Cheat! Flippin' cheat!'

'I've heard enough, Craig!' said Mr Hughes now speaking in his best loud voice. 'Give the bat to Robert and go and sit out over there!'

'I've had enough! Bent umpire! Bent! Bent!' I threw the bat at Robert West and it hit him right on the shin and he jumped up and down.

I laughed and said, 'Serves him right!'

‘Craig, you’d better go home now. I’m not putting up with that kind of behaviour!’

‘I’m not putting up with cheating! Don’t want to play in this silly game with cheats. I’m going home! It’s rubbish!’

Mr Hughes had spoken to me the next day and made me stay in at dinner time and said that I could not come to cricket practice again. And so I was going home by myself because Chelsea had gone to the dentists before the end of school.

I decided that I would go home by crossing over the stinky brook and across the fields. The fields are a large area of rough ground where there were tip heaps and it was all overgrown with long grass and weeds. To get to the fields I had to cross the stinky brook. The stinky brook was at the bottom of two steep, grassy banks. At the bottom of the bank there was a big, black, metal pipe which went across the brook. It was like a challenge to balance and walk across the big pipe. Beneath it, the stinky brook was dirty and smelly. Nearly every day the water was a different colour: black, dark red, bright green. My cousin Jimmy who was older than me, said it was because the factory further up pumped chemicals into it.

I ran down the grassy bank and just about stopped on the concrete edge of the brook. Stepping up onto the big pipe, I ran across easily without stopping. Climbing up the bank at the other side, I stopped at the top to get my breath back. When I looked up, I saw a group of boys standing near the gap in the railings where you got out of the fields. From that distance, I couldn’t see who they were so I just carried on towards the railings. When I got closer, I could see that the one at the front was smaller than the others. It was Jacob Jackson out of my class. I was just going to shout, ‘Hi, Jacob’ and squeeze through the gap in the railings. Next to him I recognised his big brother Chris. Then Chris pointed at me and said, ‘Is that him, Jake? Is that, Craig, who keeps hitting you and botherin’ you?’

'Yeh, that's him! Big mouth, Craig!'

I could see that Jacob's brother and the other two big lads were staring at me. They looked angry. One of them started thumping his fist against the palm of his hand. It was then that I turned towards the fields and began to run.

The gang ran after me. There were shouts of, "Come here, you little brat! Wait 'til we get you!" The lot of them were chasing me. I wasn't very far ahead of them when I tripped over a big clump of grass and fell headlong into a grassy hollow. When I turned over to try and get up they were all surrounding me. There was no way of escape.

'Now, you!' said Chris Jackson. 'You've been bullying our Jake and we're gonna give you a little lesson so that you will learn not to touch him again. Ever! Or else!'

'I've not done anythin'. He's a little liar! He keeps windin' me up and thumping me, so I thump him back.'

'You're the liar!' said Jacob. 'He's always at me Chris. The other week he kicked me right in my bum, in the line, for no reason.'

'Cocky little devil, aren't you? Well, we'll soon knock that out of you. And when we've finished, you won't do it again. Ed, go and get one of them nice long stems off them purple plants. I think this deserves six of the best. You like hurting other people's bottoms, so let's see how you like this just for starters!' The other big lad dragged me to my feet.

'GET OFF!' I shouted but that only made him twist my arm up my back. I knew I couldn't get away. I didn't know what to do. If only I could break free. If only there was someone to shout to for help. Shout for help. If someone could help me. Then the words came back into my mind. "If you need help, call me. Just call my name." So I did the only thing I could think of. I shouted in my loudest voice, 'Arthur! Arthur! Help! Help!'

Ed was just stripping the leaves and purple flowers from the long stem. He swished it in the air.

'Give that here, Ed! Now you lot, bend him over and hold him whilst he gets his punishment. This is what they used to do to naughty boys at school a long time ago…'

I was nearly crying and still shouting for Arthur. But I knew that it was a load of rubbish. Why should some ghost come and help me?

There was a swish and the stem hit me hard on my bum. I screamed out. It was hot and stinging. I was waiting, crying, shouting for them to stop, screwing myself up to be ready for the next pain.

I heard swishing, but nothing hit me. I heard Ed yowl out and then Chris. Jacob and the other lad had let go of me. I stood up and turned round and saw that Chris Jackson had soil on his head and face and all over his T-shirt. Jacob was jumping around knocking soil out of his hair. There was soil all over the other boy's sweat top, and Ed was bending over trying to get soil from the back of his neck.

Chris started spitting soil from his mouth. I just stood and stared. I was free. The group were scattering as sod after sod sailed through the air whacking each one of them, exploding like bombs. The sods seemed to be flying out of mid-air by themselves. I took my chance and ran as fast as I could to the railings. Looking over my shoulder, I could see grass flying from nowhere. No one seemed to be throwing them. I knew it was Arthur. I paused to laugh out loud at the scene. The four boys were all running and dancing about like them puppets on strings. They were running trying to find cover behind some of the small mounds, whilst all the time, looking towards the wooden fence.

As I reached home and went through my front gate, I still couldn't believe what had happened. Arthur had said he was my *Guardian Angel* and that he would help me. What if it was really true?

Fifteen

The next morning at school, Jacob Jackson arrived just before registration. He gave me a dirty look but he didn't say anything. He just went and sat at his table. I smiled at him. I could see that he was angry and that made his face screw up really bad. I didn't take much notice of him because I was strumming my granddad's guitar. My mum was still in bed when I was setting off for school, so I sneaked the guitar out of the cupboard under the stairs, shouted goodbye to her and set off for school, plucking at the strings all the way.

Adrian, Tom and Steven Harris were all sitting round me. Chelsea was sitting at the opposite end of the table.

'Give us a go! Go on!' said Adrian.

'My dad can play guitar and my sister does lessons at school,' said Tom.

'So can I,' I said. 'My dad showed me.'

'Bet you can't play a proper tune,' said Steven Harris. 'Go on give us a tune.'

'Bet I can.'

'Now you boys, it's time for assembly. Go back to your seats. And Craig, it's very good to see you interested in music, but you'll have to stop that now. Whose guitar is it?'

'It was my granddad's. It's mine now. Mr Dawson said in the meeting the other day that I could bring it in. And my mum let me.'

‘Well, this isn’t the time. And if everybody crowds round, you’ll end up with the strings getting broken. Let’s put it down now.’

‘But I don’t want to go to assembly. I want to play my guitar.’

‘But you can’t stay in here playing a guitar by yourself when everyone’s in assembly.’

‘I’ll be all right. I’m a big boy now.’

‘No, Craig! You know the rules like everyone else. Nobody can be inside school unsupervised.’

‘Miss Ashcroft’s the music teacher. She can come and show me.’

‘Miss Ashcroft is going to be in assembly like everyone else. She has to play the piano for the hymn. Now put it somewhere safe, then we can all line up.’

‘But some nosey, dozy little rotter will mess with it and break it.’

‘Look! Put it in my stockroom and I’ll lock it up.’

I really wanted to just play with my guitar but Miss promised me I could have it back later and we locked it in the stockroom.

After assembly I asked Miss, all the way down the corridor and up into the classroom, if I could have my guitar back. I just wanted to play it all morning. It was good just plucking and strumming. I didn’t want to do any boring English or Maths. So, I went to the stockroom door and pulled on the handle. It was still locked so I pushed against the door.

‘Can I have my guitar now?’ I shouted across the room. ‘Can I? Can I? I want to play it. Can I get the key, Miss Denton?’

‘Now, Craig, I’ve told you this is not the time. Besides…’ She was interrupted by a knock on the classroom door. Then it was opened and a lady walked in. She was carrying a big, blue file and three or four children stood behind her in the corridor. I recognised her from the meeting in Mr Dawson's office.

'There! As I was about to say, you will be going to the Group Room with Mrs Thompson and a few other children.'

'But I want my guitar!'

'Hello, Craig. Do you remember me from the meeting the other day? I said we'd be having some special group work once a week. This is going to be the first one. Come on, you can show me where the Group Room is.'

'But I want my guitar! Miss Denton has locked it in the stockroom and she won't give it me back. I want my guitar!'

'Oh, is this the guitar mentioned in the meeting?'

'Yeh. My granddad's.'

'Look, we've got a bit of talking to do and some games. I've got to find out all about you, Craig. So, at the end, if your teacher says it's OK, you can come back to class and get your guitar. Then you can show me and the others in the group what you can do. And, do you know what? I can play the guitar. I could tune it for you then. Is that OK Miss Denton?'

'Yes. When you've finished the session he can certainly come back here and I'll give him the guitar.'

'Is that a deal, Craig?'

'Yeh,' I said. 'Come on, let's get on with it!'

I went to the Group Room with the lady and four other kids, two from Year 4 and two from Year 6. The lady said who she was and told us what her job was. Then each one of us had to do the same. We had to say who we were, what class we were in, what things we liked doing best in school and at home. After that she asked about what made each of us angry and what we did when we got angry.

I did the worst things. Some of the others only did soft things like answering the teacher back and sitting sulking. Then she went on about what we could do to stop losing our temper and stuff like that. She said we could make a little voice in our head when we could feel ourselves getting angry. And this little voice could tell us to calm down and to chill out and tell us to do something nice, something better. It was then that I thought about Arthur. This is what Arthur had done. Spoken in my head. Told me what to do. And I thought, I bet none of these other kids had someone like Arthur who could be the voice in their head. I wanted to tell the lady but then I thought it was my own special secret and nobody should know except me and Chelsea. What would teachers, my mum, other kids and other people do if I listened to Arthur and didn't get angry. I bet that would make them think. And they couldn't blame me then.

When we had finished talking and done a few games which were meant to help us choose what to do instead of being angry, I said to the lady, 'Can I go and get my guitar? Can I?'

'Well, I think it'll be your playtime in another five minutes, so you'd better go and get it now.'

'Yeh, cool man!' I said, making straight for the door.

I took the guitar back to the Group Room and the lady tuned it. She showed me how to play two chords and I could do it. I kept doing it over and over. Then the lady and the other kids gave me a big clap. The bell went and the lady said, 'Now go back to your classes, ready for playtime.'

'Thanks Miss. Can I take it outside onto the playground?'

'Go back and ask your teacher and I'm sure she'll let you.'

I rushed back to the classroom. Everyone was lined up. So, I stood there and strummed out the chords, bending my legs like a pop star.

'Well done, Craig!' said Miss Denton.

'Can I take it outside to practise?'

'I don't see why not as long as you remember you can't play it when you come back in for lessons.'

Sixteen

There were four or five lads sitting on one of the benches with me. Tom, Adrian and Joe were there with Steven Harris and Ben Blackley. I was strumming the chords that Mrs Thompson had shown me. Everyone wanted a go. I gave Adrian a go and he just plucked different strings which was rubbish. He didn't even know how to hold his fingers across the strings. Steven Harris had a go and he could play a little tune on it so I took it off him because he was too good and he was showing off.

Next to us, Chelsea was playing a skipping game with lanky Lucy and fatty Lauren. The two girls were turning the long skipping rope and Chelsea was in the middle skipping and all three were singing a little rhyme. Normally, I would have pinched the rope off them and tied someone to the bars with it. Probably lanky Lucy because she was taller than me and I didn't like a girl being taller than me. Or, I would have whirled it round my head so that everyone would have to get out of my way. But I had my guitar and it was better than a scraggy old rope.

I was just playing the two chords one after another as fast as I could when a voice shouted at me.

'Hey, Guitar Man, my brother's really after you now.'

It was Jacob Jackson.

'Is he now? What – a – big – shame!'

'He's gonna do you good and proper! And if you ever touch me again you'll never play that guitar again. You might have got away this time but next time you might not have all of this little gang of yours around to help.'

'Wha'? Wha'ya' on about?' asked Adrian.

'Don't pretend you don't know. All of you. 'Cos there was more than just one who threw all them sods at us.'

'When was this?' asked Tom.

'Last night after school,' I said.

'Well, we were all at football practice,' said Adrian now sounding confused.

'And I was at my Judo lesson,' said Joe.

'Why? What happened?' asked Steven Harris.

'Well this sneaky little Jacob toady-woady was waiting for me with his big brother and two of his ugly mates when I crossed the stinky brook. They said they were gonna beat me up 'cos I'd been hitting him. So, I ran across the fields and they wouldn't have caught me, only I tripped up. Then they got me and started whacking me with one of them long stalks but I pulled away and pushed them over and ran for it. I was much too fast for them.'

'Liar, you are! Bloomin' liar. He only got away because somebody bombed us with soil and clods and sods. But wait 'til he gets you! He's gonna do you!'

'Well it wasn't us you little freak!' said Adrian and he moved towards Jacob Jackson. 'I think you need a slap or two.'

I was angry as well. That whip thing had hurt me and Jacob had called me a liar. I put my guitar down and jumped up with clenched fists. But then there was a voice in my head. "Don't bother, Craig! He's not worth it. He's just trying to frighten you and spoil your fun." I didn't know whether it was my voice or Arthur's or just a thought in my mind. But I said, 'Leave him, Adrian. He's just stopping us playing the guitar.'

I picked up my guitar and sat down again. Adrian followed me. Jacob Jackson made a few more threats, but no one was listening to him because they all wanted a go at the guitar. He went away. In a strange way that I couldn't explain, it felt better than hitting him.

'Why was he raving on about sods? Accusing us of throwing sods. We weren't even there!' said Steven Harris.

''Cos when I got away somebody threw sods at them. One went right down Jackson's neck.' I was laughing now, remembering the sight of them all jumping and dancing about with soil in their hair, on their faces and all over them.

The whistle went for the end of playtime and we all went into our lines. Chelsea caught hold of my arm as I made my way to our class line.

'Hey! Get off! Or I'll…' Then I saw it was Chelsea. 'Oh, it's you Chelsea. Did you hear my good playing? Like a pop star.'

'Yes. Those chords were OK. What was Jacob Jackson going on about?'

'Him and his brother and his weird friends tried to beat me up after school but I got away.'

'I heard that, Craig. I mean what was he on about sods for? Who threw them, Craig?'

I stopped, looked at Chelsea and hesitated. But I knew Chelsea was the only one I could tell. I knew she wouldn't laugh at me. I knew she would believe me.

'Well that big gorilla, Chris big-head Jackson, was whipping me with one of them tall purple flower things…'

'Rosebay Willow Herb.'

'Yeh, one of them. All the others were holding me and he was using it like a cane on my bum. It didn't half hurt. Then, all of a sudden these sods came flying and hit them on their bonks, down their necks, everywhere. They let me go and they couldn't see where they were coming from…'

'Where were they coming from? Who was throwing them?'

'Well, that's just it! When I reached the fence and turned round the sods were still flying at them. I didn't half laugh. They were covered in dirt. But the sods were like coming out of thin air. There was nobody around. But I know where they were coming from…'

'Where, Craig?'

'When they had hold of me I was really scared. Then I remembered what he said. He said, "If you need help just call my name." I never thought anything would happen but I just shouted "Arthur!" Then, after that the sods were coming. And I knew…'

'Knew what?'

'I knew, well, I think it was Arthur come to help me. But it might have just been a coincidence or something. There might have been a gang of boys hiding and I couldn't see them. But it might have been my mind playing tricks on me because of what he said in the Gospel Hall.'

'No, Craig! There's nothing wrong with your mind. It's not imagination. Arthur must be your *Guardian Angel*. He must be here to help you. You asked for his help and you got it. What more proof do you need than that? But we'd better not say anything to anybody else…'

Seventeen

Walking down the corridor to the classroom I was strumming my guitar.

'Everyone sit on the carpet in front of my chair, please,' said Miss Denton, as we went through the door.

Most children bobbed down and sat on the carpet. Some pushed others out of he way. Some went to sit near Miss's chair. Some sat at the back of the group leaning against the tables. But I wanted to play my guitar. I didn't want to listen to a boring story in a boring Literacy lesson. We did that every day. Same old thing. Follow Miss as she read from the big book on the easel. I hated the boring big book. Proper books are ordinary size. Most of the time I couldn't even see the words from where I was sitting and when I could, I wasn't able to read them. Then there was non-stop questions about what was happening, about words, about every boring tiny bit of it. Then at the end you had to go and do some work about it even though you'd already forgot what the story was about. So, I didn't sit on the carpet like a little kid in a nursery. I sat on the edge of the table. With my legs crossed, I supported my guitar on them and carried on playing the chords.

'Craig, put the guitar down and come and sit with everyone else.'

'I want to play my guitar!'

'I did say you could take it out to play but that, when we came in, you must put it away.'

‘But I don’t like flippin’, stinky Literacy. I just want to play my guitar!’

‘Well, you cannot do that! It is disturbing this lesson for the whole class and you cannot listen to this story and do that!’

‘Don’t want to listen to some boring story! I want to play my guitar!’

‘Craig, I said – put – it – away! This lesson is starting, NOW!’

‘No! Don’t want to!’

Miss Denton stood up and walked over to me.

‘Give the guitar to me, please, Craig!’

‘No!’ I shouted and jumped up and ran to the back of the room. I sat on the workbench top and carried on strumming. I had my special smile, which I did when I thought I’d won.

‘You cannot play that there! Give it to me!’

‘I’ll play it outside,’ I shouted. Then I jumped off the worktop, ran round the other side of the tables and holding my guitar in one hand, opened the door and jumped out into the corridor. I moved a bit further along the corridor, sat on a chair and began to play my chords.

‘Chloe, please go down to Mr Dawson and ask him to come and get Craig. Tell him he won’t stop playing his guitar,’ I heard Miss say.

A few minutes later Chloe returned, followed by Mr Dawson. I kept plucking the guitar strings and pretended not to notice Mr Dawson.

‘Craig, what do you think you are doing?’

‘Are you blind? I’m playing my guitar.’

‘How dare you speak to an adult in this school like that! It’s time for lessons, so you’d better put your guitar somewhere and go into the classroom immediately!’

‘Don’t want to do boring Literacy! I want to play my guitar!’

‘Who told you to bring that guitar to school?’

'They said I could at the meeting.'

'No, they didn't! They said if you asked everyone: me, your teacher, your mum, then you could. But you haven't, have you?'

'Don't care! I want to play my guitar!'

'You cannot do that all day! You're disturbing lessons apart from missing the lesson yourself.'

'Well, I want to play my guitar,' I said again.

'You'd better come with me, Craig.'

'Where to? You can't take my guitar!'

'If you won't go back to your lesson, you'll have to come down to my room.'

Mr Dawson came up to me and got hold of my arm. 'Come on, Craig! To my room!'

'GET OFF me!' I shouted. 'You can't touch me!'

'I'm sorry, but I can! If you won't go into class, if you are disrupting other pupils' learning, then I can certainly remove you. Do you understand? You either walk down with me or you will be carried down.'

'I'm keeping my guitar.'

'We'll talk about that in my room. But come with me sensibly.'

Inside my head I was saying, "Don't make a fuss. You can go to Mr Dawson's room and play your guitar there." So I stood up and followed Mr Dawson.

On the way downstairs Mr Dawson said, 'Now, Craig, does your mother know you've brought that guitar to school?'

'Of course she does. She said it was all right.'

'I'm sure she would have asked school first.'

I went into Mr Dawson's room and he let me sit on the fold up chair. I started strumming my guitar.

'You just sit there, Craig, I'm just popping next door into the Main Office.' And he went into the office next door.

When he was out, I noticed the camera, so I put down my guitar and went over to the controls. Moving the joystick up and down and from left to right, I could see on the monitor all the different parts of the school grounds. I zoomed in on a seagull and on the car park. I could see the number plates on the cars very clearly.

Then Mr Dawson came back in. I said, 'Look, Mr Dawson, I can see a seagull on the field. It's real big.' Before I could move he had picked up the guitar.

'I'm going to put this somewhere very safe. I've just rung your mum and she says she didn't even know you'd taken the guitar. I've asked her to come over to school to collect it. She'll be here in ten minutes. Now you go and sit in the Reception Area until she comes.'

'I want my guitar back! You can't take it!'

Mr Dawson went out through the door, holding the guitar and I ran after him shouting, 'Give me my guitar! Now! I want my guitar!'

'Sit down there and stop that! I've told you that your mum is coming and she is taking the guitar back home. So all that fuss will get you nowhere.'

'I *want* my bloomin', bloomin' guitar!' I wailed.

'Just sit down and wait!'

'I want my guitar! I want my guitar!'

'Ah, thank you, Mrs Doulton,' said Mr Dawson.

Coming through the Reception Area towards us was Mrs Doulton, one of my Learning Assistants.

'I would like you to wait here with Craig, until his mum comes.'

Mrs Doulton put an arm round my shoulder.

'Come and sit down, Craig.' I shrugged her off and sat on the floor chanting, 'I want my guitar! I want my guitar!'

Mr Dawson went off through the door and down the corridor towards his room. After a short time he returned without the guitar.

'I want my guitar!' I carried on. 'You've stolen my guitar! I'll get the police onto you.'

'Now don't be silly, Craig! Mr Dawson's just keeping your guitar safe until your mum comes,' said Mrs Doulton.

'But I want my guitar!' I screamed. Then I started crying, howling very loud and saying in between, 'I wa – wan – want my guit – tar!'

I kept repeating it. Big tears were running down my face into my mouth. I was really angry now. I screamed and thumped and kicked the carpet. I must have done this for a few minutes but nobody said anything, nobody took any notice, so I just lay there sobbing and saying, 'I want my guitar! I want my guitar!'

Five minutes later, Mum arrived. I could tell she was very angry.

'I am sorry, Mr Dawson. The little sneak took it out without telling me. I told him he couldn't take it to school without asking first.' Then she shouted at me, 'Told you! Didn't I? What did I say? You – can't – take – it – to – school!'

'Now, it's all right, Mrs Hartshorn. If you take the guitar home now then that'll solve it. There's no problem with Craig bringing it to school when we can get somebody to give him half an hour with it. You see, Craig, our music teachers are all teaching classes today. They need some notice to get off timetable. And you can't just play with it all day. You have to do your normal lessons as well.'

I was still crying, 'I wanted to play my guitar!'

'But you can't just pluck on it all day, you silly little boy. You've reading to do and Maths. Do I have to take him home now?'

'No, no! He isn't excluded. It's just that he's disturbing lessons and he wouldn't stop playing it.'

'He's like that at home. When he's doing something or watching something he likes, he won't stop for his tea or bedtime or for nothin'. I'm fed up of him!'

'Well, Craig, do you want to go back to class or go home with your mother?'

I folded my arms and plonked myself on an easy chair.

'I'm staying here! Not moving!'

Mrs Doulton sat next to me, but I wouldn't even look at her. My mum went down to Mr Dawson's room and returned with the guitar. As she went out of the door, she turned and said to me in a nasty voice, 'You lad! No more! Behave yourself or else!'

Once the guitar had gone I calmed down. It was like I was saying to myself, "There you are. What are you getting wound up for? You can play the guitar when you get home." Then I thought, "Was that me or was it…?"

After about fifteen minutes, I got up and said to Mrs Doulton, 'I'm going back to class now.'

Eighteen

It was getting on towards the end of the term. In three weeks' time we'd be finishing for the long summer holiday. I couldn't wait. Mr Dawson had arranged for Miss Ashcroft to give me an half hour lesson on my guitar once a week and a session at lunchtime. We were just starting Sports' Day heats, playing cricket and rounders in Games lessons and it would soon be the Swimming Gala.

I'd just come back from a guitar lesson with Miss Ashcroft. I liked Miss Ashcroft because she was kind and didn't shout. She showed me what to do and didn't go mad at me if I did it wrong. Miss Denton stopped the lesson and let me play a little tune for the rest of the class. I got a big clap. Then Miss gave me the key to the stockroom and I locked the guitar in there.

I sat down with my group. We were discussing different jobs and what we would like to do when we grew up. Mrs Doulton was sitting with our group.

'I want to be a fireman like my dad,' said James Baker. 'They do a very important job because they can save people's lives.'

'And what would you like to do, Leanne?' asked Mrs Doulton.

'I want to be a hairdresser, Miss. I like styling my doll's hair.' James Baker, Tony Roberts and me all started laughing. Mrs Doulton gave us one of her cross looks.

I was still laughing. Leanne Garston stuck her tongue out at us.

'Tony's gonna wash his dolly's hair when he gets home, aren't you Tony?' I started up laughing again.

'Ha! Ha! Very funny!' said Tony.

'Well, what about you, Craig?' asked Mrs Doulton.

'What?' I was ready to lose my temper because I thought she was suggesting I had a doll.

'What do you want to be when you grow up?'

'Oh! I want to be a pop star. Playing on telly with my guitar at them big concerts, like at Wembley. I want to be a pop singer just like my dad. He's gone touring round the world with his band.'

'Liar! Liar!' shouted Tony Roberts. 'Your dad's not a pop singer!'

'Yes he is, you little potato head!'

'He isn't, Mrs Doulton! He's in prison! They took him away two years ago.'

'That's enough, Tony!' said Mrs Doulton.

'You bloomin', little liar!' I shouted, and reaching across I grabbed Tony's polo shirt and pulled him across the desk. Then Mrs Doulton stood up shouting, 'Stop that, Craig!'

I had clenched my fist ready to thump Tony, but Miss was striding across the room shouting, 'Craig Hartshorn, take your hands off Tony and sit down!'

It was then that I saw Arthur standing by the door. He was smiling, but shaking his head and waving both hands down towards the floor as a sign for me to calm down. It was like pressing the pause button on a DVD when the whole action stops in one still frame. I was standing, like a statue, turned to stone for an instant. I was just like *Mr Tumnus* in the *Narnia* film turned to stone by the *White Witch,* but my fist was clenched and my arm was raised. And in that instant, which seemed to last for ages, I saw Arthur, I saw Chelsea looking towards the door, I saw Mrs Doulton looming above me and I saw Miss Denton walking towards me.

I looked at her and then back at the door. Arthur had gone. I let go of Tony's polo shirt and sat back down. My face was red and my lips were trembling. I clenched my fists again.

'Whatever is going on, Craig?'

'It's him! That Tony! He said my dad wasn't in a pop group. He said he was in jail!'

'Is this true, Mrs Doulton?'

'Craig is right. He was telling us about wanting to be a pop star when he grew up and Tony chimed in without being asked. He did say Craig's dad was in prison.'

'Well, Tony Roberts, that is a very unkind thing to say…'

'But it's true, Miss!'

'Whether it is true or not is none of your business. And you have no right making nasty remarks about other children's parents. Now, I think you should apologise to Craig.'

'Sos, Craig,' said Tony and he reached out to shake hands.

I was just about to slap his hand and go into a strop when I saw Chelsea just to the side of Miss Denton. She was nodding and encouraging me to shake hands with Tony and mouthing at the same time, "I – saw – Arthur".

So, instead, I gave a little grin, shook his hand and said in my quietest voice, 'It's OK Tony.'

'Well done, Craig!' said Miss Denton. 'I am proud of you. It took a lot to control your temper and forgive Tony. Well done!'

Nineteen

It was a hot day. I was hot and sweaty, and red in the face. My hair was plastered down wet because when we came in after dinnertime, I went into the toilets and splashed water all over my head. Now we were back outside on the field ready to do heats for Sports' Day. We were sitting on the grass listening to Miss Denton explain the events and how we would decide who should be in what event. There was a sprint running race, an obstacle race, a sack race, a relay and a long distance race which was two laps of the field.

'We will do one Girls' event, followed by the same Boys' event. And in each race the first and second to finish in each team: Reds, Yellows, Greens, Blues, will go into the race on Sports' Day.'

I put my hand up.

'Do we have to do it, Miss? I don't want to be in Sports' Day.'

'Well, normally Craig, everyone has a go and everyone in Year 5 is in the Long Distance Race anyway. So unless anyone is absent from school on the day or has broken a leg or something, then everyone is involved in an event.'

'You should be in something, Craig,' whispered Chelsea as Miss went on explaining things. 'It doesn't matter if you don't win or come second. There's nobody who can be in every event.'

'It's all right for you. I'm no good at it and I don't like it. You are good at everything.'

'No, I'm not, Craig. I'm not very good at sports and games. I've never, ever won a race or finished in the first three in Sports' Day.'

'So why do you bother, if you know you can't win.'

'It's not just about winning. It's about having a go. And perhaps one time I might just finish third or something and get some points for my team. It's not just about yourself it's about trying to help your team.'

'I don't care about no flippin' team. We always finish last anyway.'

'I've seen you running on the playground. You're a good runner. If you have a go you might just win.'

'Nah! I'm not doing any soppy Sports' Day. It's only so mums and dads can come and cheer on their own little kids. My mum never comes anyway.'

I didn't go in any event and half way through I was wrestling on the grass with Adrian and Miss shouted at me.

'Stop that messing about! If you won't take part then you must sit properly and watch.'

'But this is boring!'

'If it's boring, then you might want to go in to a Year 4 class and do some work. On second thoughts you can do something useful and come and help me to put out equipment for these next events.'

So I helped to put out the sacks and skipping ropes and benches for different events, and in the end I never went in for any event.

When we were sitting on the grass again at the end, Miss read out the names of the competitors who would be in each race. Then she said we did not do heats for the Long Distance Race because everyone would be in it.

I thought to myself, "That's what you think. I'm not going in any Long Distance Race."

I wasn't to know that watching Chelsea run in the Girls' Long Distance Race would change my mind and lead me onto other things like the Swimming Gala which would, eventually, mean the difference between life and death.

Twenty

It was hot on Sports' Day. There wasn't a cloud in the sky. Every Junior class came out and sat on their class station which was four large blue gym mats. All the classes were along one side of the running track behind a line which was about a metre from the first lane of the track. Parents sat on the grassy slope opposite us, where the football goal posts were.

I saw Chelsea's mum waving at Chelsea. My mum, as usual, hadn't come even though I'd asked her. She said, "You won't go in any races, so why should I come?" We had been allowed to bring out plastic water bottles and during the interval we were all to get a carton of orange juice. I was dressed in my PE kit like everyone else. Miss Denton had told me to change, but I only got changed because I thought it would be cooler.

At 1.30 the first of the running races began. Mr Dawson's voiced boomed out from this trumpet thing he held to his mouth. When I asked, Miss told me it was called a loud hailstone or something like that.

'The first event is the Sprint Races. Our first race is the Year 3 Girls' Sprint Race.'

I liked the look of the loud hail thing. You held it to your mouth, pressed a button and spoke into the mouthpiece. The button presser was attached to it by a twisty cable like on a telephone. Then your voice came out dead loud. When Miss wasn't looking, during the Year 6 Boys' Sprint, I worked my way to the back of the mat and quietly crawled behind the Year 4 and Year 3 classes towards the table. Mr Dawson had put the loudspeaker thing down on the table. So, I sneaked all the way across. I was just about to reach up and get hold of it when Mr Dawson said, 'Craig, what are you doing here? You should be sitting with your class. No competitors are allowed near the scorer's table unless they're handing in their finishing place card.'

'I'm not a competitor, Mr Dawson,' I said cheekily.

'Craig, no pupil, competitor, spectator or helper is allowed here without permission. And besides, everybody's in the Long Distance Race even if they aren't in any other event.'

'I'm not going in it! Can I have a go at that loudspeaker thingy?'

'If I let you then three hundred other children would all want a go. I think you'd better go back to your class station.'

'Aw, sir, I like that thing. Can I have one go?'

'Craig, go – back – to – your – class!' said Mr Dawson in a louder voice.

Then, just as the Boys' Sprint Race finished he said, 'Wait! I'll tell you what. You run in the Long Distance Race, and I'll let you announce the team scores on this.'

'I don't want to race. It's boring and I'll only finish last.'

'You might not, if you have a go. Now, anyway, you must go back.'

Mr Dawson walked me back to my class. I sat down and he said something to Miss who looked at me with a cross face. She brought me onto the front row next to Chelsea. I really wanted to have a go on the loud thingy but I wasn't going to run in the race just for that.

The races went on. Chelsea went in the Skipping Race and finished sixth. In her other race, the Obstacle Race, she finished seventh. Sitting down again she said, 'There! I told you I wouldn't finish in the first three.'

'So, why did you go in it then?'

'Just to have a go. I might have just done better and got some points. Besides I enjoyed it and my mum took some good photos.'

'You're not still going in the Long Distance Race, are you?'

'Why not? I can only try.'

'And finish last with no points again!' said Jacob Jackson from behind us. 'Your girlfriend's a loser! I wish she wasn't in Blues. Spoils our scores. I wish she was in some other team!'

'SHUT UP! Leave her alone! She did her best. I bet you don't do much better!'

'Well, yes I did, actually. Second in the Sprint, second in the Sack Race. That's four points! And I'll probably finish second in the Long Distance. And she'll be last!'

I grabbed hold of Jacob's T-shirt. I didn't care about his big brother.

'I said SHUT UP Jackson! Leave her alone!'

'Shut up yourself! At least she's got some bottle! You won't go in anything, big chicken Craig! You'll get no points! Zero points, Craig!'

'You little creature!' I shouted and pulled Jacob over.

'Now, what's going on there?' said Miss, suddenly.

I let go of Jacob's T-shirt. 'Nothing Miss Denton. Just a friendly argument about which team will win. I say it'll be Reds.'

She didn't believe me, because she moved Jacob Jackson to the other side of her.

It was time for the Long Distance races. Then Mr Dawson said on his speaker:

'Would all competitors for the Year 5 Girls' race, please come to the start.' Chelsea got up to go to the starting line.

'Wish me luck, Craig.'

'What? To win?'

'No! Wish me luck that I'll finish the course.' Then she picked her way through the seated kids and went off to the start.

Two laps of the field was a long way on such a hot day. All the way round, Chelsea was at the back. When it came to the last lap she was more than half a lap behind the winner. Everyone had finished and Chelsea came into the straight all by herself, in last position. She was red in the face and was running so slowly that she was nearly walking. As she came towards the finish, all alone, people were shouting and cheering and clapping.

Miss Denton shouted, 'Keep going Chelsea! You'll do it! Well done! Keep going!'

So I shouted, 'Come on, Chelsea! Come on!'

Looking across the track to the parents, I could see everyone was standing up, cheering. Chelsea crossed the finish line and there was the biggest cheer of the afternoon. Teachers and children and her mother ran to congratulate her. Her mother came up to her as she was bent over, puffing and coughing and trying to get her breath. She gave Chelsea something. And when Chelsea put the blue object into her mouth and pressed it, I knew it was an inhaler. I never knew that she had asthma.

As she left the finish line and came back towards our class station, I got up and ran to her.

'Well done, Chelsea! You made it!'

'Th – thanks, Craig.' Then Jacob Jackson was there.

'Yeh, made it! Last!'

My face turned angry and I moved towards him. Mr Dawson announced,

'Year 5 Boys' Long Distance Race. Please report to the start.'

Then he turned and made for the start. Turning back he shouted, 'But at least she did run. Not like some chickens I know!'

It was then that I knew I would run in the race.

'Don't listen to him, Chelsea. He's a goof! I'll see you after. Won't be long!'

'Wh – where are – you – going?'

'I'm gonna have a go in the race. We'll see how good Jacob Jackson is.'

As I turned and looked across the track I could see Chelsea's mum just sitting down again on the grassy bank. And for a fraction of a second I saw, standing behind her, Arthur.

I said in my mind, "I'm scared, Arthur. Scared. Scared of finishing last. But I've got to try. Got to!"

Twenty-One

All the Year 5 boys lined up at the start. There were about twenty-five of us. It reminded me of the start of the *Grand National* when all those horses try to get in one straight line. We were all pushing and moving to get in a good place. I was already sweating in the heat. There were movements in my tummy. My mum said it happens when we are nervous and they were called butterflies.

Mr Dawson shouted, 'On your marks!'

We all put one foot forward on the line. I was feeling really scared. I wanted to walk away and go and sit down. It was much better just sitting and watching. Then there was a voice in my head saying, "You can do it, Craig!" Not long ago I would never have questioned that it was anything but thoughts in my head but now, I didn't know if the voice was mine or Arthur's.

'Get set! Go!'

I was hesitating, but was carried forward with everyone else. Half way round the first lap, just by the rugby posts, I felt hot and exhausted. I wanted to stop running. I was gasping for breath. I was in the middle of the group. Two runners overtook me, so I tried to speed up. My chest was hurting and I got a sharp pain in my side. I just wanted to stop and sit down but, as we came into the finishing straight for the first time, everyone was cheering and shouting. Out of the corner of my eye, I saw Chelsea standing up. She shouted, 'Come on, Craig! You're doing great! Keep going! Keep going!'

Then I heard a small group who must have been in my red team chanting:

'Craig! Craig! Craig!'

Somehow it made me carry on. As we crossed the finishing line for the first time, I passed Adrian and Ben Blackley. Adrian looked across at me, but he was red in the face and too tired to say anything.

Starting on the second lap I was in about tenth place. Then the sharp pain in my side went and I could breathe a lot easier. I was hot and sweat dripped off my nose, but I wasn't feeling too bad. I tried a little sprint and went past three others. Ahead of me were a group of six. As we came to the rugby posts again Luke Jones was about ten metres in the lead. And in second place was Jacob Jackson. Jacob Jackson had made me angry when he said nasty things about Chelsea. I was going to punch him in the stomach when Miss stopped us. Now the anger came back but I couldn't lash out at anyone or scream or shout. I could only run. I half closed my eyes, pumped hard with my arms and ran as fast as I could. My breathing was heavy and I thought my chest would explode. At the top bend, turning into the straight, I ran past the chasing group on the outside. In front of me was only Luke Jones and Jacob Jackson. Luke Jones was the best runner in the school even though he was only in Year 5. He went to a Running Club.

Now people were cheering, standing and jumping up and down. But I couldn't hear a sound. All I could hear was the voice in my head. "Go on! Keep going! You've got to catch Jackson!" I was running faster and faster. My legs were hurting, my chest was hurting, sweat was all over my face and neck and back. But I put in one big effort. Half way down the straight, I overtook Jacob Jackson. With a surprised look on his face he tried to speed up. But I had gone past him and he wasn't going to catch me. Twenty metres from the finishing line I was catching Luke Jones. Ten metres and I was just behind him. Three metres and I was drawing level with him. Then Luke Jones lunged forward at the tape to win the race and almost touching his elbows I sprawled over the line and fell headlong onto the grass. I had finished second.

Mr Hughes helped me up. He put a second place card in my hand. I was bending over spitting out onto the grass. I felt like being sick. Then the noise came back to my ears. Shouting, cheering and chanting. Red team in every class were on their feet chanting, 'Craig! Craig! Craig!' I stood up, red in the face and sweating. I was still breathing very fast.

Mr Hughes said, 'Well done, Craig! Good run!'

But under my breath I said, 'What's good? I only finished second!'

Walking slowly, I went to the Scorer's Table and threw my card down. Mrs Abel said, 'Two points for Red.'

Head down, I walked away to go back to our class. Then Luke Jones stood in front of me.

'Good run, Craig!' He was breathing heavily. 'Another metre and you'd have beaten me. Who do you run for? Which club?'

'None,' I said. I was still a bit sulky.

'None? A good runner like you. Tell you what, you'd have beaten quite a few in our Under 12s. Why don't you come down and join us? You'd do really well. We train every Tuesday and Thursday from 5.30. Joe, our coach, would welcome you with open arms. Go on. Come down. You'd like it. You'd like the lads down there. It's only at the High School Sports' Centre. It's nothing to join.'

'I'll – er – I'll think about it.' I was feeling better. Second wasn't so bad after all. Then Mr Dawson came up and said, 'Well done, Craig! What a good run! Second to Luke Jones. You know he trains every week. They have a good Athletics

Club up at the High School. You should join it. You'd do really well.'

'Thanks,' I said. 'I might.'

'Have you forgotten?'

'What?'

'I promised you could announce the scores if you ran in the race. Come back to the table after the final Year 6 Long Distance Race.'

I smiled even more and walked with my head up back to my class station. Kids all the way along shouted, "Well done!" and chanted "Craig! Craig!" again.

Chelsea met me and said, 'Well done, Craig! I knew you could do it. Remember what Arthur said, "Don't be scared", you can only do your best. And look what you did.'

'Well, I'm not…' I stopped. I was going to say "scared". I was going to be cocky. But instead I said, '… I mean – I was scared, and I thought I couldn't go on; I wanted to stop, but you – you didn't, you never stopped, so, I couldn't and – and I saw Jacob Jackson in front and I didn't feel scared. I was angry at him and all I wanted to do was get past him, and I did, but I didn't win so…'

'So, nothing, Craig Hartshorn!'

The last two races were run. Mr Dawson sent a Year 6 girl to Miss to say he wanted me to go to the Scorer's Table.

'Now, Craig, it's your turn to announce the final scores. Just read these scores in the order on this paper.'

Then, in front of everyone, I spoke on the loudspeaker thing. My voice seemed to echo all round the field.

'In fourth place with 186 points, Yellows.' A big cheer went up and everyone clapped, 'third place with 190 points, Greens.' Cheers and clapping followed again. 'Second place with 207 points, Blues.' Big cheers, 'And in first place with 208 points, the Red Team.'

All the Reds jumped up and down and shouted and cheered and punched the air.

The Sports' Cup was presented to the two Red Team captains and they ran up the middle of the track with all the Reds following them, including me.

As we went back inside, Chelsea said, 'See. You didn't win. You finished second. You got two points and your team won by one point. If you hadn't run, your team wouldn't have won. You did it for yourself. You did it for your team.'

Twenty-Two

The summer term was coming to an end. In the week, after Sports' Day, each year group went to the baths to swim in the Year Group Galas. I had been going to the baths nearly every week with my Social Worker and I could swim two lengths, probably more.

Last year I wouldn't enter because I was only a learner and all the learners had to go in the one width Beginners' Race. I didn't like that. I didn't want to be the winner of a Beginners' Race. But now I could swim much better and after Sports' Day, I felt a lot more confident. So I entered the Boys' Freestyle and, I won!

During the last two weeks of term, I'd been down to the Running Club and everyone was pleased to see me. Luke had told Joe about me. We did lots of sprint drills and single laps of the track. We played lots of running games and by the second or third session, I was beginning to keep up with everyone. On the last Saturday of the term, we had a Fun Day at the Running Club and it was brill. There were lots of stalls, bouncy castles, trampolines and fitness tests to play.

During these last two weeks, I'd also been going to Chelsea's house and she helped me read some of the Running Club's news sheets and newsletters. With her mum, they showed me how to work out sounds and read words from "Flashy Cards" (I think they called them).

At school we had class exchanges to meet our next year's teacher. Our Year 6 teacher for September was Mr Hughes. Then we had the School Play, *The Wizard of Oz,* the Leavers' Assembly and, on the last day, the Final Assembly. Next year we would be Year 6 pupils and we would be leaving for the High School next July.

In the last week of term, Chelsea and me went to the Gospel Hall quite a few times but Arthur never appeared. We thought he must have done his *Guardian Angel* job, because I had not been in real trouble for a while. I escaped exclusion in the last week for bringing in some eggs and throwing them out of the window. They splattered really well on the footpath to the playground: a lovely yellow mess. But I said sorry to Mr Dawson and I had to clean it all up with a mop, a bucket and a hosepipe with the caretaker, Mr Forbes, watching over me. I had also been doing some good things like the Running Club, instead of messing about. So, we thought he must have gone to wherever he had to go. But how wrong we were. By the end of the summer holiday things were to happen which meant I needed him more than ever. He was still around. It was as if he knew that he would still be needed.

Twenty-Three

The summer passed quicker for me than it had ever done before. Usually I got bored and went round with a gang looking for something to wreck. In the first week, I kept going to Chelsea's house and we played in her garden and I did some reading and writing and drawing and painting. We had drinks and biscuits, and twice I stayed for tea. My mum wasn't bothered, because she was never in. She was always at the Bingo.

Then, in the second week, Chelsea and her mum went on holiday to Spain for a fortnight. During the whole six weeks I never went anywhere with my mum. Not even shopping in the Town Centre. So, I went with a gang of lads. Jimmy Rogers nicked three bags of crisps from a shop. They wanted me to nick some sweets, but I wouldn't. Usually I would have done so that everyone would think I was big and hard. But somehow I didn't feel like that anymore and I knew that what they were doing was wrong. So, I wouldn't. Even when Jack Taylor said I was a chicken. I just went, 'Cluck, cluck, to you!' and he didn't bother. Then, Jonathan Pearce got nabbed trying to rob some bottles of pop. We all ran off. The police were called and he was taken home to his mum and dad. They warned his parents that if he did any more stealing he would be in real trouble.

It was then that a voice came into my head telling me to keep away from the gang because all they wanted to do was get in trouble. It couldn't have been Arthur, I thought, because he had gone. It must be me.

I decided to keep going to the Running Club because they never wanted you to do things which were wrong. And it was more fun. My Social Worker got me into a Holiday Club and we had games and activities. Once we all went on a trip to the zoo and then we went to an adventure place. It was great. We climbed things, swung on things, went on the "*Death Slide*" and crawled through tunnels.

When Chelsea came back she had bought me a present. It was a box of Spanish toffees, and I shared them with her. They were the nicest toffees I'd ever eaten. During the next two weeks, I often went to Chelsea's house and her mum organised lots of games for us. We had a badminton set and a set of balls where you threw one and then each person had to throw balls to see who could get nearest. Chelsea's mum told me it was a French game and what it was called, but I can't remember the name. She also had a multi-coloured parachute that she used at the playgroup where she sometimes went. We played games with it, going under it, going over it and using it to keep a ball in the air. We threw large plastic darts with rubber suckers on their ends at a target. I asked my Social Worker if Chelsea could come to the Holiday Club sometimes. She arranged it, and Chelsea went with me three times. I think she enjoyed it especially on the day we went to the adventure place.

The holiday passed. The last week had come. It was the Monday afternoon. Chelsea's mum was working at the playgroup. I didn't know where my mum was or what she was doing. We decided to go to the Gospel Hall again. The sun was really strong. At first, when we climbed in through our secret panel, it was dim and dusty. As our eyes got used to it we could see millions of little bits of dust moving in the rays of the sun which came in through the back window. I kicked a piece of brick across the floor and shouted, 'Arthur, are you there? Arthur!'

No answer.

'Arthur!' called Chelsea. 'Does Craig still need you, or have you finished your work here?'

No answer.

I turned away and looked to see if there was anything to mess with. Then Chelsea's hand was on my shoulder.

'Craig, look!' She was whispering.

I turned round quickly.

'What?' At first I couldn't see anything.

'There! In that patch of light.'

I looked, following her pointing finger. And there was Arthur. Very faint. You could see the wall through him. He was all wobbly and almost disappearing all the time.

'Are you still here then? I don't need you anymore. You better go to where you should be, instead of squatting here,' I said. Then I laughed at my own joke.

Arthur spoke. His voice was soft, very quiet. It was like the volume on the remote control was turned down. It was like he was walking away into the distance and his voice was getting fainter, harder to hear.

'One more thing to do,' he said. 'For you to show your love. For you to help Chelsea. Don't be scared.' Then he faded and was gone.

'I'm not scared! Not scared! Not anymore! Don't you call me scared…'

'Craig, we're all scared at times. You know that. And you know that when we face what we're scared of, like when you went in that race, and you thought it would be too hard, that's when we have to push away the fear. But what does he mean? How would you help me?'

'Dunno. Search me!'

We went back to the Gospel Hall on Tuesday and twice on Wednesday, but he never appeared.

Chelsea said, ‘Perhaps he was saying he had to go. That was the one more thing he had to do for us. That you’d, we’d, be all right now without him. That we had to stick together to help each other. Perhaps *‘Someone Up There’* has decided that he has done his job and he can move on from here.’

‘I hope you’re right. Glad he’s gone! Good riddance!’

But Chelsea was wrong. She wasn’t to know that I would need him because she would need him a great lot.

Twenty-Four

It was Thursday. There were only two full days of the summer holiday left. Then it was the weekend. Then it was back to school on Monday. Mum had bought me a new school sweatshirt and white polo shirt.

I called on Chelsea just after dinner. Her mum had gone to the Playgroup to get it ready for a new lot starting on Monday. There was no Running Club and my Holiday Club had finished.

We were moping about in her back garden and getting a bit bored. Then suddenly I said, 'I know let's go down to the fields. It's great for exploring. You can make great dens there. And there are some good trails.'

'My mum doesn't like me going there. She says it's dangerous and there can be odd folk around. She says that brook is dangerous and I'm not a good swimmer.'

'I've been loads. There's no trouble. Besides I'm with you. It's only like going in the Gospel Hall. That's more dangerous. It could fall down any time. And we won't go near the brook.'

In the end Chelsea agreed, and we set off. Little did we know what was about to happen. And I still blame myself. It was my idea and it was me who persuaded Chelsea to go.

Squeezing through the gap in the railings, I ran away from the stinking brook towards the fields. Chelsea followed me.

I stripped lots of leaves from the tall stalk plants and threw them at Chelsea. Laughing, she did the same and we had a mock battle. She chased me down a trail into the fields. I didn't realise that Jacob Jackson, his big brother and gang were making a den. It was too late when we nearly ran into them.

'Well, look who it is!' said Chris Jackson.

'And with his girlfriend as well,' said Jacob.

'Don't we owe him somethin'?' He carried on. 'Getting his mates onto us. Ambushing us. I think a lesson is overdue.'

I just stood, mouth open. For those seconds, I couldn't move. Chelsea stood just behind me. She was pale and frightened.

'Where's your mates now?' said one of the others. 'Or is this girl gonna do your fighting this time?'

Jacob raised the long stalk spear in his hand. 'Beat me in the race, eh! Sneaked up when I didn't know. Well, I'll owe you for that as well.'

As he threw the spear I grabbed Chelsea and shouted, 'Run!' We turned and began to run back the way we had come. The spear hit the back of my leg but we were already dashing through long grass, nettles, the beds of tall, purple-headed flowers. The gang behind were shouting and whooping. After a short distance, Chris Jackson grabbed the back of my shirt. I tried to pull away and knock him off but instead he flung me round and I landed in the long grass. Jacob jumped on Chelsea and pulled her down. She screamed. I tried to get up, shouting, 'Jackson, get off her! You…' But Chris Jackson pinned me to the ground. The others helped to pull us both up and held us, twisting our arms.

'GET OFF! GET OFF! Leave us alone or else…'

'Or else, nothing!' shouted Chris Jackson. 'You got away last time, but now we have you. Two for the price of one. And you're gonna get some of your own medicine. Some nice juicy sods! Right lads, get pulling some sods.'

'Wait! Wait!' said Ed. 'I've gotta better idea. Remember that film we saw the other week, *Pirates of The Caribbean*, well, they made troublemakers walk the plank. Why don't we make these two walk the pipe, over the brook? And see if they can dance to a little bombardment of sods.'

'Great idea!' shouted Chris Jackson. 'Come on, bring 'em along me hearties!'

'Aye, aye, Cap'n!' shouted the others together, laughing as they did so.

They dragged and pushed us along.

'Don't! Please don't! I can't swim!' Chelsea was sobbing.

They took no notice.

I shouted, 'It's nothing to do with her! It's me you want! LET HER GO!'

'Very brave! Looking after girly friend,' said Jacob in a snidey voice.

'Anyone who crosses the Jackson Gang gets double trouble back. So, stop whining!' Chris Jackson thumped me as he said it.

We were dragged down the steep bank. I went on my bottom, but they still pulled me down. The stinking brook was running grey and murky.

I was put up on the end of the pipe. Then two of the gang each held onto one of Chelsea's arms and pulled her up onto the pipe, making her balance. Jacob had collected a pile of sods and was picking one up.

I was thinking of calling for Arthur again. But I thought he'd gone and I was panicking, trying to think how I could help Chelsea get off the pipe. I wasn't bothered about myself. I knew I could just run along the pipe quickly and escape up the other bank. As we stood balanced on the end of the pipe, they peppered us with sods.

'Walk! Walk!' shouted Chris Jackson.

I walked quite easily out over the water. Chelsea edged nervously, shaking and crying. I turned back and held her hand. Sods exploded at our feet.

'Go on ye Landlubbers. Move or die!' shouted one of the gang.

A sod hit me on the side of the head. There was a loud cheer from the Jackson Gang. Soil ran down my face and neck. I nearly overbalanced. I pulled Chelsea towards me. I knew we had to get across as fast as possible. I knew Chelsea couldn't keep her balance if sods hit her. We were now nearly in the middle.

'Come on, Chelsea! To me! Come on! Quick as you can! If we get across we'll be all right.'

Then a sod hit Chelsea at the back of her legs. She pulled her hand away from me. More sods splattered around her feet. I was reaching forward trying to grab her. She seemed to try and jump to avoid the sods and that's when she slipped, falling first onto the pipe with her back, then hitting her head and then falling into the water. I was grasping at thin air. Chelsea disappeared under the water.

'You dirty, bloody scum!' I shouted. 'You…' But I couldn't say any more. I was frantic with fear. Chelsea's head surfaced and disappeared again. The current swept her along to the tunnel which went under the road. I couldn't think. I just jumped in. The water was cold and stinking. It went over my head. I surfaced again quickly and started to kick my legs and move my arms as fast as I could. The current was carrying me forward.

'Bloody hell!' came a shout from the gang. 'Let's get outta here!'

As I looked for Chelsea, the gang scrambled up the bank and were soon out of sight.

Then I saw her arm and hair on the surface just near the tunnel. I swam hard towards her. She disappeared again. Then her head bobbed up about three metres in front of me. Water splashed everywhere as I kicked my legs like a madman. We were in the tunnel, and I grabbed her sweat top. I pulled and her shoulder and head came up. I remembered the Water Safety and Rescue lessons I'd had at the baths. I went on my back, turned her over and held under her chin so that her face was above water. I used the breaststroke leg kick to get to the bank. At the other side of the tunnel there were no concrete edges and the bank was lower. I was able to stand up. The water was up to my waist. Then I dragged her half up onto the bank, climbed out myself and pulled her onto the grass. She was pale and her lips were purple. I didn't know if she was breathing.

I was panicking now. Slime and mud and dirty water were dripping off my hair into my face. I began to shiver with the wet clothes clinging to me. I was angry. I was shouting. I was thumping the ground. I was frightened. Was Chelsea dead? And once again I realised my temper and anger could not help me. I had to do something. Fast. Then I remembered the mouth to mouth thing I'd done at the baths. With one hand on Chelsea's forehead, I tilted her head backwards, pinched her nose between my other finger and thumb and opened her mouth. Then I gave her mouth to mouth breathing, counting and stopping and starting again like I'd been shown. After what seemed like ages, I heard her cough then there was a gurgling sound. "Turn her on her side", something said in my head. "On her side." Then I remembered what they called the Recovery Position. I turned her onto her side and water and sick came out of her mouth. I felt her chest moving slightly. She was breathing. I knew Chelsea had not opened her eyes. She had not woken up. I knew I had to act quickly. I knew I needed help. Leaving Chelsea on her side, I ran up the grassy bank shouting:

'Help! Help!' At the top, I ran out onto the path and made for the wooden gate which was the entrance to The Brook Walk.

Two men were standing at the bus stop on the pavement. One had a mobile phone to his ear.

'Mister, help… My friend's fallen in! She won't wake up! HELP!'

Startled, they both turned round and when they saw me dripping with the black water and slime on my hands and all over my face, they immediately turned and came through the gate.

'This way! Down here!'

The two men got to the top of the bank and saw Chelsea lying, not moving, on the edge of the brook.

'Jimmy, call an ambulance on your mobile,' said the first man in a frightened voice. Then he ran and slid down the grassy bank.

'I've given her mouth to mouth and water and stuff came out.'

The man felt her pulse and put his ear to her chest.

'Still breathing. Can feel a pulse.'

Then he turned Chelsea onto her back and gave her mouth to mouth again. When more water and muck came out he turned her back onto her side. He took off his sweat top and wrapped it round Chelsea's body.

'Is she going to be all right?' I asked, now beginning to tremble and shiver with shock and cold.

'She's breathing. She's got a heartbeat. But she's still unconscious. Did she hit her head on anything? THINK... We'll need to tell the paramedics when they get here.'

'Yes, yes. We – we were on the pipe. Some big lads made us cross and – and – she slipped and fell on the pipe and then in – I think she banged her head on the pipe…'

After what seemed like hours, I heard the siren of the ambulance. The man on the bank with me shouted up to the other man to show the ambulance where we were.

'Tell them she's breathing, but is unconscious. The boy thinks she banged her head.'

The ambulance men brought a stretcher and oxygen equipment. They quickly examined Chelsea and put a mask on her and a silvery blanket. Then she was put on the stretcher and taken up to the top. One of the ambulance men put a silvery blanket round me and I was put in the ambulance too.

Outside, as they were closing the doors, I heard the man who had come down the bank say, '…The boy jumped in and rescued her. Gave her mouth to mouth straight away. Otherwise, I think she'd already be a gonner…'

Twenty-Five

My mum came rushing through the curtain of the cubicle. I was sitting up on the bed dressed in a hospital robe. They'd examined me and questioned me and given me a hot shower.

'Craig, Craig!' she shouted, putting a plastic bag full of my clothes on the floor. She grabbed hold of me and hugged me.

'*Blood and Sand*! Thank God you're all right! They told me you'd been in the brook. That you saved Chelsea. What happened? How is she?'

'She's still not come round. They've got her in a special room, but they won't let me go and see her, so I don't know…'

'Now, there! Don't you be worrying. She'll be in Intensive Care. They'll be looking after her. They'll only let her mum in there.'

'Is her mum here?'

'Yes, Craig. I saw her in the corridor, but when she saw me she didn't look too pleased. Probably so worried. They took her to see Chelsea. She was really upset so I didn't say anything. But what were you doing down at that stinking brook. You know what I've told you…!'

Now she was wasn't worried about me any longer. She just wanted to tell me off, as usual.

'But we didn't go there. We only went to the fields. It was Jacob Jackson and his loony gang who got us and made us go across the pipe. They threw sods at us. Bloomin' sods! And

Chelsea – Chelsea fell in…' And all the tears suddenly came running out of my eyes. I couldn't stop crying.

'It's all right now. You'll be all right. Chelsea will be OK.'

I calmed down a little bit.

'But this is ridiculous. It's not bullying, it's like – like gangsters. Why should they do that?'

'For – for nothing!' I said trying to get my breath and stop crying. 'Probably because I beat Jacob Jackson at Sports' Day and probably because I got away, when they tried to get me before…'

'But why were they trying to get you, Craig?'

My mum was always looking for something that I had done wrong. They'd made Chelsea fall in the brook and somehow my mum wanted to see if it was my fault.

'They were!' I shouted. I could feel myself getting angry again. 'Because that stupid, goon faced Jackson is always bugging me at school! Winds me up and when I do it back to him he tells his big baboon of a brother.'

'Are you sure you haven't done anything nasty to this Jacob Jackson?'

'Only what he does to me! Calls me names so I call him back. Kicks me under the desk, so I kick him back. And he tells Miss and she always blames me.'

'That's flippin' well bullying. Well, I'll be up at that school on Monday. They soon phone me up when you've done anything wrong. And this is far worse than anything you've done! We'll see what Mr Dawson says about this!'

The hospital let me go home with my mum. They wouldn't let me go and see Chelsea. On Friday I just sat in all day and played on my *PlayStation* and worried about Chelsea. I didn't know how she was. I couldn't do anything.

Mum came into my room.

'Are you all right, Craig?'

‘Yeh,’ I said quietly.

‘Do you want anything?’

‘No.’

‘You’re very quiet. Too quiet, Craig. I know you’re worried, but all we can do is wait and, as they say, pray. It’s out of our hands.’

“It’s out of our hands.” Those words went round in my head. I was helpless. I was angry inside. I couldn’t do anything. “It’s out of our hands.”

‘Would you like a Mars ice cream? It’s your favourite.’

‘No.’

Normally I would have lost my temper and shouted at my mum when she kept pestering me and asking how I was. But now I couldn’t be bothered. I didn’t want to talk. I didn’t want to do anything. I just wanted Chelsea to be all right. I just wanted to see her running and laughing.

‘Are you sure you don’t want anything?’

‘No. Just to know how Chelsea is.’

‘Well, I can’t stand this. I’m going to ring that Chelsea’s mother and find out. You’d have thought she would have rung us. I can’t see you moping about all day. She’ll be at the hospital, but I’ve got her mobile number somewhere. The one you gave me.’

Ten minutes later my mum came back. She was upset and red in the face.

I was suddenly frightened.

‘What’s the matter, mum? What’s happened?’

‘It’s that woman. Chelsea’s mum. Snooty cow.’

‘What did she say, mum?’

‘Chelsea’s still unconscious. I said we’d like to come and visit. She said – she…’

I could see mum was really upset.

‘What mum? What?’

'She said it'd be better if we didn't go – under the circumstances of what happened…'

'What does that mean, mum?'

'Well, Craig, she thinks it's all your fault. She blames you for taking her – taking…'

'It was my idea. If I hadn't gone on about going then – perhaps…'

'No, Craig!' My mum was shouting and crying. 'No! Not this time! I'm not having it! It was you who saved her! It was! You can be a pain, I know that! And most of the time it is your fault, but not this time. That gang of hooligans are to blame, plain and simple! If it wasn't for you, risking your own life, that girl would be… I'm not having it! You're not taking the blame for this!'

Then Mum went out of the room with her face in her hands. I had never heard her cry so loud before. I didn't know what to do. Chelsea still not awake. Her mother against me. My mum crying. And "It's out of our hands." But whose hands was it in then? Whose? What could I do? I could only think of one thing, Arthur. But he had gone. Chelsea had said so. He had gone faint and disappeared. What had he said? "One more thing to do." One more. Not the last. One more. For me. For Chelsea. That's what he said. Was Chelsea wrong? Had Arthur known what would happen? He had one more thing to do. That's what he said. And I knew there was something I could do. I knew there was one chance. I knew I had to go to the Gospel Hall. One more time. I knew I had to try.

I found mum in the living room. She was still wiping her eyes with tissues; for the first time since I can remember, I sat on the sofa next to my mum and put my arm round her shoulder.

'It's all right, Mum. Don't cry.' Before she had tried to stop me from being upset. Now it was my turn to stop her from being upset.

'Don't worry! It's only because Chelsea's mum's really upset. What if it was me lying in the hospital and I wasn't waking up? What if it was me, and I might never wake up…'

'I know, Craig. I know. She must be going out of her mind. She said it was touch and go. Said Chelsea might not – might not…' She started crying again. This time for Chelsea. Then. '…But it wasn't your fault, Craig!'

'Mum, I need some fresh air. I need a break. Can I go for a walk?'

'Yes, of course you can. That's a good idea. Take your mind off things. But be back for your tea. We'll have something nice. Pizza and chips.'

Twenty-Six

I stood in the long grass and stared at the Gospel Hall. Since we'd first met Arthur, a lot had happened. He had said I was scared. I looked at the building, in the bright afternoon sunshine. I was scared. Scared that Arthur wouldn't be there. Scared for Chelsea. I didn't want to go in, yet at the same time, I couldn't wait to go in.

Fat shafts of sunlight criss-crossed in the gloom of the Hall. I walked to the middle of the floor, mortar and rubble crunching under my feet. I stood still. There was a silence. No birds. No cars. Nothing. Silence. I felt alone. Scared.

'Arthur!' I shouted. The word echoed and then disappeared into open spaces above. Silence again.

'Arthur! Are you there Arthur?'

Silence. Then a creaking. I looked round. The door to the passage was moving slightly. A breeze coming down the passage was blowing the door.

'Arthur! Please!' I shouted. 'I need your help. We need your help. Me and Chelsea. Please help her. She mustn't die. You can help her. Your one more thing.'

Still nothing.

So, I tried again.

'Please, Arthur! I said I didn't need you. I said you'd better go. I'm sorry. Really, proper sorry. I was wrong. I said you were just a squatter. And it doesn't matter if you were. I'm just an idiot. I do need you. Not for me. For Chelsea.'

I was clenching my fists hard. Tears began to run down my cheeks into my mouth. I crouched down. My hands were wiping away the tears. I was gulping and gasping for words.

'I'm sorry, Arthur! I'm sorry! I wasn't nice to you. And you were right. I'm scared, Arthur. I'm really scared. I've never been so scared in all my life. You said I was scared and I tried to do better and I will do better. I will! But I'm still scared.'

I crouched and sobbed. I was all alone. Then I heard the voice. It was very quiet. I held my breath so that I could hear.

'But this time it's different. You're scared for someone else, not yourself.'

I looked up. There was no one there, but the air in front of me seemed to glow. It was a strange, bright light.

I stood up, hands at my side, staring in amazement at the bright glow.

'Help Chelsea. Please. I'm sorry. I try to be good but I'm just bad. If you help Chelsea, I'll always be good.'

The glowing light vibrated with the voice.

'Craig, remember this. We've all got good and bad in us. We just need to find the good. Let the good win. You're letting the good win. Let love win. Your love has helped you and Chelsea, and me.'

Then the glow went fainter until everything was normal again. Somehow I seemed calm again. I could sit still and think and be happy.

Twenty-Seven

We had no news about Chelsea on Friday or Saturday. On Sunday my mum rang the hospital. They told her that Chelsea's condition was stable but still critical, that she had not woken up.

Monday was the first day of the new school year. I said I didn't want to go back to school, not without Chelsea. Mum said that I had to go. That I couldn't just mope about all day. That school would take my mind off it. That all my class mates would want to ask about Chelsea. None of these things made me want to go. But when she told me that one of the Learning Assistants had bumped into her in the supermarket and told her that on Monday there would be a Special Assembly for Chelsea, then I knew I had to go. She had said there would be special prayers for Chelsea. Even the local vicar was coming into the assembly to say prayers for Chelsea.

It was Monday morning. Kids were talking in registration about things that had happened in the holiday. There was a lot of talk about Chelsea. I was very quiet. A few kids asked me about Chelsea. Jacob Jackson wasn't in school. My mum had come to school with me before nine o'clock to see Mr Dawson. I sat in the Reception and she went down into Mr Dawson's room.

Ten minutes later Mr Dawson came to get me. Once I was sitting in the room he said, 'I've listened to what your mum has said happened. I want to tell you what I've told your mum.

I am going to have a meeting with Jacob Jackson and his parents. I can only deal with what happens in school. And if things from home start to cause trouble in school then I will take action. First of all your teacher and myself will monitor what goes on. There is to be no name calling, fighting or trouble of any kind between the two of you. Should Jacob start any bother then you must report it immediately to your teacher and me. I will be saying the same thing to him. What happened on Thursday is very disturbing and I have told your mum it is outside the powers of the school to deal with, so I do not want any come back in school. But your actions were very brave and you should both be proud of what you did. I am, and so is the whole of the school.'

Later mum told me that Mr Dawson had said it was perhaps a matter for the police and that she should inform them. She did, later, make a complaint to the police.

Usually everybody was excited and chattering when they went into the first assembly of the new school year. But this first Monday morning was different. Sad music was playing on the school stereo system as everyone filed into the hall in silence. Teachers spoke very quietly to children. The vicar sat at the side. Mr Dawson looked serious.

Mr Dawson said "Good Morning" to everybody and then he began.

'Welcome back on this first day of a new term, a new school year. It is in this first assembly that we usually think about a new start, a fresh chance to do our best. But, today, sadly, we must think about the tragic event which happened on Thursday. Thankfully all of you here are back at school, fit and healthy and safe, looking smart in your new uniforms, ready to begin a new school year. Our new Year 6 are sitting at the back of the hall ready to start their final year. All except for Chelsea. Many of you may know about the accident which happened on Thursday. And now our thoughts and prayers must be for

Chelsea and her mother. At present she is in Intensive Care in the hospital and has not yet regained consciousness. We must pray for Chelsea. We must ask God to help her to recover so that she can be back at school again. And we must thank God for the bravery and quick thinking of Craig Hartshorn, who risked his own life to pull Chelsea out of the water. Craig showed an extraordinary presence of mind to give mouth to mouth resuscitation and to get help.'

I had not expected this. My mum or someone must have told Mr Dawson. Normally, I would have felt good, big, the best, to be called a hero, but I could only put my head down trying to stop the sobbing noise coming out of my mouth. I wiped wetness from my eyes and fiddled with my shoelaces. I kept my head down knowing that everyone was turning round to look at me.

'I have asked Reverend Williams to join us today to lead us in our prayers. So, put your hands together and close your eyes.'

Reverend Williams strode to the centre of the hall. He said a prayer to help Chelsea and all those who were ill or suffering in hospital. I never joined in with prayers in assembly before. I never usually even closed my eyes or listened. But now I held my hands together tightly and kept my eyes closed. At the end of the prayer, I joined in with the Amen.

Then Reverend Williams said, 'Keep your eyes closed because I want you to say in your head, your own prayer for Chelsea. You all know Chelsea better than me. You'll all have some personal thoughts about Chelsea. Think hard about her, and ask God for His Mercy.'

My mouth was straight and my teeth were pressed hard against each other. I squeezed my eyes tight shut. In my mind I said, "Please God, please help Chelsea get better. Please get Arthur to help her. He said he was my *Guardian Angel* and had to help me. I need his help. I need Your help. I don't need

Arthur now, for myself. Just let him be Chelsea's *Guardian Angel*. Please make Chelsea wake up. Please make her better. I will be good. I will do my best. Thank you God. Thank you Arthur. Amen.'

It was the first time I'd ever said a prayer. My mum had said prayers were useless because there was no God. But I said this prayer and knew that He was there, because Arthur was there. I knew he would help me.

Twenty-Eight

That day at school went slowly. I didn't really do anything. I didn't do much work. I didn't talk to anyone. I sat quietly thinking, hoping, praying. At break times I sat in a quiet corner. Not even Adrian or Tom could persuade me to join in the game of football. They didn't try too hard. They seemed to know, that I wanted to be left by myself.

At the end of the day, I went straight home. I had tea but I didn't eat much. I was sitting upstairs playing on my *PlayStation.* I couldn't really be bothered with the *Formula1* racing game. I kept crashing my car on every bend. Something which I never usually did.

Then at about half past five there was a knock on the door. I heard my mum asking someone to come in. Probably Mary, I thought. Then mum was calling up the stairs, telling me to come down. I came down slowly, with my head down. Halfway down I looked up. And standing in the hallway was Chelsea's mum. My heart suddenly began to go faster and faster and I was really scared.

'Craig, Chelsea's mum has something to tell you.'

My heart began to beat even faster. I quickly went down the last few steps. I looked at Chelsea's mum, dreading what her face would be like.

But she looked calm. She wasn't frowning. She looked like she did whenever I played at their house. A little smile came onto her face.

‘Craig,’ she said. Then she paused. ‘Craig, Chelsea’s going to be OK. She’s awake and chatting away. She is just like her old self.’ The smile spread across her face.

‘Really – you mean – she’s…’ I couldn’t get the words to come out of my mouth.

‘Yes. She’s better.’

I couldn’t help myself. I made a whooping noise and began punching the air with both fists.

‘Oh, what great news! We are so glad!’ said my mum.

‘But, Craig...’

I let my arms drop to my side. I thought, as it usually does to me, that bad news was coming.

‘Craig, I’ve come to apologise to you and your mum. Chelsea has told me everything. I was nasty to your mum, I thought it was all your fault. I needed someone to blame. I thought you had taken her to that brook. And all the time it was you who saved my daughter’s life. It is you I need to thank, not to blame. You must have been feeling awful and I didn’t help in that. So, thank you Craig. Will you forgive me?’

I could only stand and nod and smile.

‘We’ve reported the incident to the police and the names of the boys involved. It’s in their hands now,’ Mum said.

‘I’m going to visit Chelsea now. Mrs Hartshorn, could Craig come with me? I’ll have him back by about eight thirty. Chelsea can’t wait to see him. She’s been pestering the life out of me, since she woke up.’

‘Of course he can.’ And, so, that evening I went to visit Chelsea.

When we walked into the ward, Chelsea was sitting up. She looked her old self. She smiled and shouted across the ward to me. Sitting at the bedside, we chatted away. If Chelsea said thanks once, she said it a dozen times. Then there was question after question. How did she fall into the water? Did she go right under? How did I get her out? When she’d finished with that, she asked about school and what had happened and what was Mr Hughes, our new teacher, like. And all the time I could tell from the excitement on her face, the way her eyes were darting from left to right, that she had something to tell me, a secret.

Then, at last, she said, 'Mum, I'm feeling thirsty. Could you please get a drink from the hospital shop?'

'Of course I can. I'm being stupid. I'm getting in the way and I can't see it. You need some time together to chat. I'll not rush back. I'll probably get a cup of tea in the café.'

As soon as Chelsea's mum had gone through the door I said, 'What's the matter? I know you've got something to tell me. What's happened?'

'Well, it was Arthur, I think.'

'What was Arthur? What about him? What?'

'It was when I was unconscious. It was strange. You might not believe me. But, I know it happened…'

'What happened? What?'

'I was looking at myself lying on the bed with tubes coming out of me everywhere. I was standing at the bottom of the bed looking at myself. I was unconscious and as white as a ghost lying on the bed. But, at the same time, I was standing at the bottom of the bed and I felt all right. Then slowly I went up...'

'Up? Up where?'

'I went up to the ceiling. Kind of floated. I looked down on the whole thing. Me in the bed. Tubes, monitors bleeping, nurses. And then it went black.'

'What went black?'

'Everything. Complete blackness. But I was travelling through it very fast. Away from the bed, the room, the hospital. It was like flying through space. Then, suddenly, there was a bright light. Not like a light in a house, or daylight, or sunshine. I can't explain it. I can't describe it. It was more like pure silver. I knew I was leaving myself on the bed. I knew I was going to a new place. I wanted to go to the place, but I also wanted to go back to my mum, to you, to all my friends. It was then that I saw a shape form in the light. It was the shape of a person. But I couldn't make out the face or anything. Then, from this light, an arm stretched out. A voice said, "Take my hand, you've got to go back." I thought I knew the voice but I couldn't place it. I took the hand and we rushed into darkness as the light got smaller and smaller. It was then that I woke up in the Intensive Care Unit. It was then that I knew I'd heard the voice before. I knew who it was…'

'Arthur!' I couldn't wait to say it.

'Yes. It was Arthur's voice. He brought me back.'

'I asked him, Chelsea. He never appeared but I asked him.'

Chelsea was about to say something but she suddenly stopped. Her mouth was open and she was staring at something over my right shoulder. Quickly I turned round.

Arthur was standing there, brighter than we'd ever seen him.

'Arthur!' I said. 'Thank you! Thank you! I never believed in you at first, but now, I do. Thank you!'

'My job here is done. Be happy. Don't be scared. Don't be scared to show your love. That's what has saved Chelsea and you. I have helped you, and Chelsea has helped you, and you have helped both of us. Now, I must move on. Goodbye.'

Then the thinning light of Arthur seemed to break up, like pixels on a computer screen, like white diamonds or tiny stars and in one long wave they rushed out from the bedside and up to the ceiling and disappeared.

Twenty-Nine

They kept Chelsea in hospital for the rest of the week. I went to see her nearly every evening.

Then, when she came out of hospital, I went round hers to play and keep her company. In between I'd started back at the Running Club and I was doing really well. At school Mr Hughes said he was going to give me and a few others some extra lessons after school for an hour, in reading and writing. Normally I would have refused but I never forgot what I'd promised Arthur if he'd help Chelsea. And besides, I got on well with Mr Hughes and I decided I was going to do it for Chelsea, and my mum, and myself.

By the end of the second week Chelsea had still not come back to school. I was doing really well at reading and writing. I began to like the classes because the reading and writing was getting easier and I realised that I could do it. I was getting in less trouble, possibly because Jacob Jackson had been put in the other Year 6 class and so we couldn't bug each other. I only saw him at break times and he was very quiet and didn't come near me. My mum told me that the police had visited the Jacksons and that they had been cautioned. I didn't get to know if anything had happened to them and I didn't care as long as they kept away from me. I was becoming friends with Luke Jones. I went to his house for tea one afternoon after school and we had a great time. I'd say Luke Jones was now my best mate. And I never argued with him or played nasty tricks on him or thumped him or anything.

It was one Wednesday evening after school, only three weeks before half term, and I was at Chelsea's house. She had still not come back to school. I had been reading a few pages of my reading book to Chelsea who was dead impressed with how well I was doing, when I suddenly decided to ask the question which had been bugging me over the last four weeks.

'Chelsea, I was – well, I was wondering, you've not been to school yet. Are you still not really better? Is everything OK?'

Then Chelsea had a funny, nervous look on her face.

'I've been meaning to tell you, Craig, but, it's hard…'

'What? Are you all right?'

'I'm OK Craig. Fighting fit. It's just that – just that – at half term we're moving.'

'Moving? Moving, what?'

'Moving house. We're going to live down south.'

'What? You can't. What?'

'I'm sorry, Craig. You see my mum has been upset by everything that has happened. She doesn't like some of the rough boys round here…'

'Like me, you mean!'

'No! Never you! You're not one of them. You're better than that, and don't you forget it. My mum really likes you and – and, so do I. But all this has scared her. But, more than that, she's met this man; we were with him in Spain. Since dad died she's been all alone. And now she's met this really nice man who lives down south. They're going to get married and we're going to live with him.'

I was upset. I didn't know what to say or do. I was getting angry. But I knew I couldn't do anything. And then Chelsea smiled, and in a strange way I was happy for her. I said, 'Then, you'll have a dad…' There was a tear in the corner of my eye.

I felt like crying but I knew I mustn't, I knew I couldn't in front of Chelsea. Chelsea seemed happy and I didn't want to spoil it for her.

Chelsea said, 'Yes.' Then she paused and said, 'How's your mum?'

'OK. Much the same. But she doesn't shout at me as much.'

'Perhaps, because you don't get into as much trouble.'

'Yeh, perhaps. But, my dad, you know, he's not in a pop group. I just wanted him to be. He's – well, he's in prison.'

'I know, Craig.'

'You know! Who told you?'

'Everyone knows.'

'And you were still my friend?'

'Why not? You're Craig. Nobody else.'

Changing the subject she said, 'How are you getting on at the Running Club? How are you getting on with Luke Jones?'

'Luke!' I said, 'Luke's a good mate. After you he's my best mate. I'm going to his party at half term.'

'I am glad, Craig. But, when I leave, you'll not forget me, will you?'

'I'll never forget you, Chelsea. We'll always be best mates. But – well – I'm going – going to – miss you.'

'I'm not going to the far ends of the earth, you know. Once we're settled in, mum has already said you can come and visit. If you want to.'

'Course, I'll come!' I said, feeling a bit better. 'Try and stop me!'

'And I'll be coming back up for visits. My Uncle David and Aunt Jess and my two cousins Louise and Paul live round here. Look, give me your mobile number. When I get down there, mum says she's getting me a new mobile. As soon as I get it I'll ring you. See how you're getting on. See if your top of the class.'

And we both laughed, as we had done many times before.

I went home that evening feeling down.

Half term came and Chelsea and her mum moved out. By the end of half term, a big removal van was parked outside Chelsea's old house and new people were moving in. I went to Luke Jones' party and it was the best ever. At school and after school we went everywhere together. But, from time to time, I still thought about Chelsea and the Gospel Hall, and Arthur.

Thirty

I often sit, in quiet moments, and think, "I had a *Guardian Angel*, but I don't know if it was Arthur or Chelsea".

Perhaps it was both.